T0366093

THE LOST HEIR

THE LOST HEIR

MONICA JENKINS

authorHOUSE®

AuthorHouse™
1663 Liberty Drive
Bloomington, IN 47403
www.authorhouse.com
Phone: 1-800-839-8640

© 2012 by Monica Jenkins. All rights reserved.

No part of this book may be reproduced, stored in a retrieval system, or transmitted by any means without the written permission of the author.

Published by AuthorHouse   10/12/2012

ISBN: 978-1-4772-8165-9 (sc)
ISBN: 978-1-4772-8164-2 (e)

Library of Congress Control Number: 2012919502

Any people depicted in stock imagery provided by Thinkstock are models, and such images are being used for illustrative purposes only.
Certain stock imagery © Thinkstock.

This book is printed on acid-free paper.

Because of the dynamic nature of the Internet, any web addresses or links contained in this book may have changed since publication and may no longer be valid. The views expressed in this work are solely those of the author and do not necessarily reflect the views of the publisher, and the publisher hereby disclaims any responsibility for them.

I would like to dedicate this book to my brothers and sisters, as well as my parents.

I would also like to dedicate this book to, two of my many supportive teachers, Mrs. Willet, and Ms. Brockman.

Additionally I dedicate this book to my many great friends who have supported me and encouraged me to keep writing.

All of these people are very special to me. They have inspired me to do my best in everything I do and to never give up.

Without them this book wouldn't be possible. So to them, I give special thanks.

136,614 B.C.

It was a beautiful day outside, we hadn't seen many days like this so we decided to have a picnic. We were all outside playing magic ball when we heard a terrifying scream. We all stopped and looked in the direction toward the castle; there was an explosion and more screams. I turned back to them quickly and told them to run. I knew she had returned; it was only a matter of time. I had to protect them no matter what. As they scattered into the woods I prepared myself for a battle. She burst through the doors followed by hundreds of hybrid-serpents. They were deadly creatures. She stared at me for what seemed like eternity before she attacked, and I knew I was going to die.

CHAPTER I

P resent day:

It was dark, and yet I could see everything like it was daytime. I had heard rustling noise and roars. I ran. Then there were tortured screams and loud bangs and something exploded in the distance. There was no end to this misery. They wouldn't stop. Not until I gave up. But they were crazy to think I would give up now. I turned around and walked into the middle of a war, the war between good and evil, light and dark; the age old story. Of course this time the dark and evil was succeeding. I had the upper hand, had more people, more soldiers, more creatures to fight for me. Of course I wasn't going to give them half of what I had promised them, but that was part of battle strategy. You have to make them believe that you will stand by your cause. Of course no one ever does. And I mean ever. So when I gained power over the dimensions of course I would have to appoint a general and commanders to help me with the entire kingdom but that's fine because either way my name would be stamped in the history books. Then I heard a tortured scream; then I realized it had come from me.

I suddenly woke up; all I knew was that it was early. I didn't realize exactly what time it was until I looked at my alarm clock that was ringing on my nightstand. "Oh no" I said. It was already

6:00 am. I had to get up now or I was going to be late for school. That's just great. All I needed was to be tardy on my first day back. I jumped out of bed and ran over to my closet. Great no time to pick out something that matched . . . . but I didn't care, I just had to hurry. So I grabbed a pair of blue jeans and a t-shirt and pulled it on over my head as fast as I could. Before I left I grabbed my neck to make sure my necklace was still there. Although I have never taken it off, I stilled checked to many sure it hadn't fallen off on its own. I ran down the stairs, grabbed an apple . . . . on my way out the door I yelled "love you mom, I'm going to a friend's house after school, I should be back around 7 okay?" I didn't have time to wait for a response, I had to go. So I slammed the door shut and ran down the sidewalk.

I live about a block away from my high school so I usually walk to school, but today I had to run . . . it was a good thing I had taken track last year.

I got to school just as the bell rang so I ran down the hall . . . all the sudden I hear "Mackenzie, you're not supposed to be running in the hallway" crap. "Busted" was all I could think. Just as I stopped the bell rang, crap. I was already tardy. I got my detention slip from the teacher who had caught me running in the hall. Went to class and as soon as I walked through the door I had another detention slip shoved in my face. This was going to be a long day.

CHAPTER 2

After class my teachers Mr. burrow said "Mackenzie, I would like to have a word with you please." I turned to Britt and all I could say was "crap" she laughed and said she'd save me a seat in our next class. We have 5 of 7 classes together. As the last student left the classroom Mr. Burrow started talking "Mackenzie this is getting to be a regular thing with you, I don't like to give you detention but you leave me with no choice." This was a typical speech I got from my teachers; I've already had this talk with four of my other ones. Since I already knew how this would turn out I said "I know Mr. Burrow I try my hardest to get here on time, but lately I haven't been getting very much sleep. I'm really sorry for being late, I'll try my very best to make sure it doesn't happen again." Mr. Burrow frowned deeply but said "all right, and maybe you should see a doctor about you not being able to sleep." Great, another thing I needed an appointment with the doctor for. Ugh I hate doctors' offices. Besides I already have medicine for not being able to sleep well.

After my little talk with Mr. Burrow I ran to Mrs. Kerry's class. I walked into her room a minute before the tardy bell rang. Thank god. I took my seat beside Brittany. We sat together in every class we had together. So I made it through 2nd period and up till 4th period I didn't get into any trouble. But when it was time for 4th period I was tardy again but this time I just got a warning. I've already had about 6 warnings in this class.

Before we left to go to lunch I stopped by my locker. I put in my combination, and as I pulled my locker opened a note fell out. I bent down and picked it up. As I opened it I read:

> *"I've been watching you Mackenzie JO Delemorte' or as your family and friends call you, Max. I know a lot about you, you have many moments when you think you're not like everyone else. And I can assure you you're not. In fact you are very different from your classmates, as is your mother. If you want to know more, come find me . . . I will tell you everything you need to know. I will see you very soon.*
>
> *Ms. Crane"*

I threw the note down on the floor and screamed. Who was Ms. Crane? How did she know all of that? Has she been watching me or something? Who else knew about this? And most importantly, what did she want?

CHAPTER 3

I turned to Britt in shock . . . . what had I just read? Was it a threat or was it some kind of promise? I didn't care either way, if the point was to scare me it certainly worked. Brittany asked "what is it? What does it say?" I bent down but stopped before I picked up the note . . . should I? I momentarily hesitated but I picked it up anyway. I handed the note to Brittany and she read it out loud . . . . when she was finished she looked as if she was a deer in the headlights. "Max, do you know anyone named Ms. Crane? And what does she want?" she asked me the exact same questions I just asked myself. The sad part is I don't know anyone with that name. Well at least I don't think I do.

I put the note in my pocket. The Brittany and continued on our way to the cafeteria. We weren't the most popular people in school but we had a lot of friends. As we opened the doors, Tyler and the others that sit with us waved us over. As we sat down Jake, another one of our friends asked us "Where have you two been? We're having pizza for lunch; I think most of it might be gone. So if you want a slice you better hurry." "Thanks, but I think we're good" Brittany said as she looked at me. "Yeah I'm good" I said.

After lunch me and Britt was on our way to our 5th period as she said with excitement "wait a minute, that note might not be to you Max." She was right it could have been to anyone, but the fact was, it wasn't. "Britt, can I come over to your house after school? Wait, I have to go to detention" I asked as she laughed and said "That's great cause I've got detention too, I mean when you wasn't in breakfast I kind of figured that you would have it so I took the liberty of getting it too." She was smart I had to give her that. I told her that she was amazing . . . . then we split up to go to our 5th period classes.

CHAPTER 4

When it was 5:00 I was so relieved. Then I remembered I had to tell Brittany about the note. Right about that time Brittany sprinted up behind me and screamed "Hey you! Wait for me!" man could she be annoying sometimes. I stopped and waited for her to catch up, and then we were on our way to the student parking. I got my license this year, exactly two weeks after my birthday. I loved my car and even though it was a hand-me-down I was still excited to have one. Then again I'm not very picky. A car is a car.

When we got to Brittany's house we went up to her room. Then I started the conversation "hey uh . . . . do you remember that note?" I asked.

"Yeah it was really creepy" she sad

"I think that I want to find out who she is . . . I mean if she knows something about me that I don't then I want to find out what it is"

I couldn't believe what I was hearing. Did Max really want to find this woman? The way she was talking, I'm pretty sure she did.

"I don't think that I understand" I said in shock.

"I think that I want to find Ms. Crane. She might know something"

"And what could she possibly know? Huh" I said with disgust.

"My mom has always been a little secretive. And I want to know why. And if this Ms. Crane knows why then I want to find out. We've been friend since we were in diapers. I honestly can't believe you don't trust me on this!"

Ouch. That hurt. But she was right we have been friends a long time. And I mean if I was the one wanting to find out more about myself let alone my mom, then I would want her to trust me as well.

"I do trust you; it's just that we don't know who she is. For all we know she might be some kind of serial killer or something. That put aside, how would you even find her anyway?" I asked. At that second she really looked kind of excited, confused and there was something else there that I couldn't quit pinpoint.

"Okay, you're right. How would we find her? Do you know anyone whose last name is Crane?"

"No I don't think I do, I don't remember ever hearing that name before"

Was Brittany really agreeing to this? I never thought that she would. But now I have a bigger problem, neither of us knows anyone with the last name Crane. I don't know how I will find her . . . . but I sure will try my hardest.

"Okay, well after I leave here I'm going to go to the library and see if they'll let me look through the old archives."

"Alright, well when are you leaving?"

"I don't know maybe in about an hour. I have to be home before 7, if not mom will freak"

"Your right, hey if you want to get to the library and have enough time for the archives you better hurry"

"Okay" I said, knowing Brittany was right.

I left her house and got into my car. When I got to the library, Scott was about to lock up. I ran over to him yelling "Hey Scott, wait for me!"

"Oh hey max, I'm sorry but the library is closed"

"I know that, I came to see you" man I felt bad for lying to him. I just hope that he catches on.

"Oh okay, why?"

"I wanted to know if . . . . if you wanted to go out with me sometime?"

"I didn't know you liked me"

"Yeah well I'm usually shy . . . . Britt told me I shouldn't be such a coward"

"You're not a coward . . . . you're just you"

"Gee thanks" I said

"No I mean, I didn't mean it like that, that's all. I like you to, I just always figured someone like you wouldn't go for someone like me"

"What do you mean someone like me?" I asked defensively

"Someone, beautiful, funny, sweet and just you"

"Awe, thanks and I would love to go out on a date with someone like you" I said as I offered a small smile.

"Thanks, so you really want to get into the library that bad huh?"

"Yeah kind of, but I really would like to go out sometime"

"Oh okay, what about Friday? I could pick you up at 7 o'clock . . . ad I'm supposed to close tonight but I guess it wouldn't hurt to be open for another hour or so."

"That sounds great and thank you so much"

"You're welcome, so what exactly are you looking for?"

"Actually I need access to the archives. I need to find my birth certificate, and find out where my mom's from"

"Okay, that's easy. Follow me"

CHAPTER 5

We went to the back of the library and went through a small door that said 'Archives'. We started looking through the first filling cabinet that held birth certificates labeled M-N. We looked through every folder but there was no birth certificate that said Mackenzie Jo Delemorte'. So then we decided to look through the folders for all the last names of Delemorte'. Again we found nothing. After we gave up on that, we looked for my mom's family tree since I didn't know my father's name. My mom's name is Geneva Elizabeth Delemorte' so we looked through the entire filing cabinet labeled G-H. We found nothing. "This can't be right; maybe we are looking in the wrong section or something. This doesn't make any sense, how can there be no record of my birth or my mom's family tree. She's never been married so Delemorte' is her maiden name. Why can't we find anything?" I asked Scott on the verge of tears.

I don't know, but trust me it'll be alright. I'll look tomorrow when I come in during the afternoon. Okay? Calm down, I don't like seeing you all upset" he said.

"You don't? And thank you for all your help."

"No I don't, and you're welcome. And since I don't want you driving while you're upset why don't we go out for ice cream? If it'll make you feel better I will even buy it too"

"you're such a dork, how are you going to offer me ice cream and then say you'll buy it if it'll make me feel better?"

We left the library and went downtown to the ice cream parlor. I sat down at the table as he went to order. The parlor had always been my favorite place to come as a kid. It was decorated in a funky 70's theme. Everything was red, white, orange, and yellow or red and white checkered. Scott bought us a giant ice cream sundae to share. It had fudge, caramel, strawberries, whipped cream, and sprinkles. As he sat back down I asked "how did you know that this is my favorite ice cream place?"

"I didn't, but I do now" he said smiling.

"So then how did you know that ice cream sundaes are my favorite kind of ice cream?"

"You told me in the car remember?"

"Oh yeah, sorry I forgot" I said blushing. Man I felt stupid now.

"It's okay, we all forget sometimes, so why do you suppose we didn't find anything?"

"I don't know? It was the strange though" I said scooping a big bite of ice cream into my mouth.

"Yeah, it was strange. Maybe you should ask her when you get home huh?"

"Yeah . . . . I think I'm going to do that."

We stayed at the ice cream parlor until at least 8:00 then Scott drove me back to the library to get my car. Right before he had left he had gave me a kiss on the cheek and told me to be careful. He was sweet; I had to give him that. As I left the library I saw a white crane fly overhead. I didn't know if I was imagining things or if I really saw it. But I wasn't about to wait to find out. I got in my car and drove down the road after the bird.

CHAPTER 6

I was probably a mile out of town at this time. Just as I was starting to think that I was just imagining things the bird disappeared. "Crap!" I said, now furious. Then a young girl appeared in the middle of the road. I had to swerve to miss her. As I went sliding off the road into the ditch I jumped out and ran over to the young woman.

"Oh my god, Are you okay? I didn't see you, do you need an ambulance? If you do I have my cell phone in the car and I would be more than happy to call one for you"

"I'm fine dear. Honestly I am. I have been looking for you"

"Me? Are you sure you're okay?"

"Yes, I'm okay; my name is Ms. Crane, like I said a moment ago. I have been looking for you"

She was just as beautiful as her mother. I just hope that I haven't scared the poor child. It is important that she trust me if my plan was to follow through as I hoped it would, but first I have to make sure she don't trust the people around her.

"You're Ms. Crane? I can't believe it; I've been looking for you. Then I saw the crane and had a feeling that if I followed it that I would find you. I'm sorry, was that kind of weird?" she asked, I could tell that she was confused.

"No dear that was not weird at all, honestly I meant for it to be that way. I'm just glad that you caught on and followed the bird." I told her hoping that she wouldn't realize what I had just said.

"What do you mean, you meant it that way?"

"If you will follow me, I will show you." I told her gently.

"Show me what exactly?" she asked a little confused.

She asked a little confused.

"Have you ever heard of mythology; you know like unicorns, dragons and things like that?"

"Yes. I'm reading a book on mythology right now"

"Okay, well then it's safe to say that everything you've ever been told about mythology is real, besides the fact that it's not." That's all I could tell her for now.

"Okay, this is getting a little weird, and for some odd reason I feel like you're telling the truth, so where exactly do we go from here?"

"A place that you would only hear about in a fairytale"

"O . . . k I guess, can we go now?"

"Alright, it's over here. And please try not to ask so many questions, unless you feel that you absolutely have to"

"Oh alright, sorry"

"Don't be dear; it's not your fault that you're naturally curious. We all are most of the time"

I didn't know who this woman was but I felt like I could trust her more than anyone else, and I had just met her. She was mysterious yet in a way so obvious. I couldn't help but notice how young she looked. She had blonde hair specked with touches of brown. She had bright blue eyes that made you feel welcome. Her skin was a beautiful olive color and her teeth, when she smiled were perfect. She was wearing a white t-shirt and blue jeans. She didn't even have wrinkles; the only thing that made her seem old was her voice and the way she spoke. I was overcome with curiosity at this point but when then I remembered what she said 'try not to ask so many questions, unless you feel you absolutely have too'.

"We are here." She said in a gentle voice.

"We are where? I don't see anything except this massive tree"

"I know, but that is how it was made to appear"

She moved her hand across the tree and a spark of bright blue seemed to encircle the trees trunk. I couldn't believe what I had seen at that moment.

"Is that some sort of door? But how, it was . . . it is just a tree trunk"

"I told you my dear that is how it was made to look. It keeps me and everyone on the other side safe from intruders"

"Other side . . . what do you mean other side?"

"You'll see in just a moment. Follow me and stay close"

As I followed her through the door I felt a strong emotion hit me. It was like fear or terror. I looked around but all I could see was tree's bushes and houses that were either burned halfway down or entirely. I felt as if I had just stepped into some sort of horror movie. I was scared; I had to admit that, even if I had only admitted it to myself.

"Yes dear, we are all scared but now you are here. And that means the prophecy is coming true."

"What prophecy? What do you mean we . . . there is no one else here."

CHAPTER 7

She turned away from me and began to say something instead she just started walking. As I followed I felt more like an obedient child doing as she was told. I was confused now, and even more curious. I had to know where we were going and just as I opened my mouth to ask, Ms. Crane said "we are going to the refugee camp, where you will meet with a few others and they will examine you as well as ask you questions."

"Examine me for what exactly?"

"I was going to wait to tell you but first I have to ask you a few things"

"Go ahead. I will answer them as truthfully as I can, I promise" I said happily.

"I know you will. Alright, have you ever felt like you hadn't belonged on earth?"

"Yes, always, I just didn't seem to fit in anywhere and I've always felt odd being around my friends and even my mom"

"Have you ever made things happen that you couldn't explain things that just happen out of nowhere? Things that are totally as you would say cool?"

"Yes I have, almost all the time but they only seem to happen when I have a strong emotion, but there's always something different." I said feeling a little bit confused now.

"Alright then I have the right girl, if you are ready then I will tell you why I brought you here. But you have to promise me that you'll listen to them with an open mind, and heart ok"

"Ok I promise"

The look on her face had turned very serious now. I could tell that this was not going to be easy, especially since she had to ask me those questions first, I don't even know why I told her about it. I mean I haven't even told Brittany let alone my own mom. And just then she started to talk.

"138,625 years ago the first queen and known prophet Queen Mariana, was being attacked in her own castle. She didn't know the woman who had attacked her but she had heard of her and knew she was dangerous. She tried her best to get back to her bed chambers to create her first and only daughter. She poured all her magic into an egg and put her amulet around it, and whispered something to the egg. Then when this woman finally got to the queen, she murdered her. When she tried to destroy the egg she was burned, she didn't know that the amulet was protected with ancient powers; the amulet would protect anyone who wore it . . . as well as anyone and anything around it. It was truly amazing. But it made the woman furious; she decided that when the egg hatched she would then destroy the one who hatched from it."

"Wow, that amazing but what does it have to do with me? Wait, you're not saying that . . ." I asked her in confusion.

"Oh dear, I don't know if you are or not, but you do have abilities you have yet to understand"

"No, I have no abilities; I'm a normal teenage girl. I should have to worry about breakouts not magic" I told her with the most serious voice I had.

"But you do have abilities, you always have. They are very special, you can try to deny it all you want, but it's who you are and it will always have an effect on you no matter where you are or where you go. And even wherever you live."

"Okay, well let's say I do; which by the way I am not agreeing to, where will I start? I don't know how to use it; heck I barley know how to make my own breakfast" I said furiously, although the whole breakfast thing was kind of an exaggeration.

"It will come to you naturally. I'm not saying it will be easy but it's a start. And you will have teachers and tutors to help you"

"But I don't even know how to use them! I mean don't they come with some kind of control manual or something?"

"No my dear, they do not. But when a close friend of your mothers examines you, they will better understand it. And they will help you just as they helped your mother."

"Wait, that's another thing . . . . I have a mom, you know the woman that gave birth to me. The one I've been living with my entire life"

The mother you know is not yours. In fact she is your mother's sister. She took you away as soon as she heard who was in the castle"

"So you're telling me that my mom is actually my aunt? That's not true . . . . that can't be true!"

"But it is. It is probably the truest thing that you'll ever hear"

"Why are you doing this to me? Just leave me alone and stop lying to me!"

CHAPTER 8

I don't know why but my eyes started tearing up. I didn't want to hear any more so I ran past the woman and didn't stop. I was running and running and I felt as if someone was following me. I bet that it was Ms. Crane but as I stopped to see who it was, something big and dark flew over my head. I was terrified at that moment, and for a split second I thought I was hallucinating. But I knew I wasn't. I was terrified and anxious at the same time. I had no reason to be, but I was. All I knew anymore was that I just wanted to go back home, to the quiet little town of Ackerman. How was I supposed to believe any of this? I don't know, but I do know that magic is not real. This had to be some sort or illusion or something. Some kind of alternate reality, I just needed to find the switch and turn it off. I was freaking out of so I took off running, I didn't even get a few yards away from where I was when a dragon swooped down over my head. I started to run away from it but t had turned around and was flying right at me.

CHAPTER 9

The last thing I remember after that is falling from a good distance and hitting my head on something hard.

When I woke up, I was scared and I didn't know where I was so as I jumped up I fell off the side of a bed. As I sat up on the floor and looked around I saw a beautiful wooden bed that had a red comforter that had a golden design on it. As I got up off the floor to take a closer look at the designs, I realized that it was the same one I wore on my necklace. It was a crescent moon with a single star hanging from the tip of it. The pillows had the exact same design on them as well. Stunned, I decided to take a look around. It was a fairly large room it had three massive stain glass windows the two smaller ones on the sides of the biggest one which was in the center. The two smaller windows each had a single star in the center of them. The biggest one and by far the prettiest had the same designs which were showcased on the bed, pillows as well as my necklace.

I walked around the rest of the room. The room was furnished with the beautiful bed, which was fit for a queen. A perfect pearl white vanity that had twelve drawers, six on each side, each had a golden handle. On the top of the vanity placed perfectly in the center was what looked like a jewelry box; I'll be sure to check that out later. There was a large table that lined the back wall of the room with red, white and yellow roses.

On one wall there were two giant double doors, each one gold with red lines in a hypnotic from painted on them. I walked over and opened them. There were beautiful dresses hung up, and beautiful shoes lined the bottom of the closet. There were five podiums spread out below the dresses, each one had a crown with five points. Each point topped with a red ruby, a red ruby also rested in the center of each of them. The main crown was silver, and had diamonds all over it. The largest crown was in the middle and the smaller crowns spread out on either side of the crown.

"Wow . . . this is amazing" I said quietly to myself.

That's when I heard a knock on the door. I jumped, decided that whoever brought me here didn't need to know that I was awake, so I shut the massive doors as quickly and quietly as possible, and ran over to the bed and laid down the exact way I was when I woke up.

"Excuse me . . . are you awake yet?" a man asked, and then there was a paused before he started again "No answer . . . well um anyway I'm sorry for bringing you here, I didn't mean to frighten you. My name is Artemis, you seemed like you were scared so I decided to bring you somewhere you were going to be safe."

CHAPTER 10

I f this guy was telling the truth; that he thought I was in danger then I shouldn't be afraid. Should I? No, I shouldn't. If he was kind enough to save me from a beast then he shouldn't mean me any harm. Quite frankly the only thing that he's done wrong is try to keep me safe. I got up and walked over to the door, and opened it up just to see him walking away.

"Uh, hey" I said, shocked to find that my voice came out a little hoarse. He spun around and started to speak then paused.it looked like he was still gathering his thoughts when he said "Hello, so uh, do you like your room?"

"Yes. It's perfect. I love it" I said smiling so big that my cheeks hurt.

"Good, so would you like to join me for dinner?"

"Sure would, I'm starving. So what are we having?"

"Actually we're having a dinner in honor of you"

"So then we're having pizza and fries?"

"What is this pizza and fries you ask for?"

"I guess you don't have that here huh? Well pizza is pretty much dough made into a circle, with sauce, cheese and whatever other toppings you wanted baked in an oven. Fries are potatoes cut into slices or wedges, whichever one you prefer and fried in oil. There not very good for you but they taste good."

"How interesting, we must try this pizza and fries sometime"

"Sounds great" I said

"Oh and we are having dinner with family and friends, something like what your people call a thanksgiving dinner."

"That's cool I guess"

"Why don't you wash up and get dressed for dinner"

"Okay . . . but I'm already dressed"

"Yes, but you are not in the right attire. I am positive you've seen the dresses. Am I correct?"

"Yes sir, which one do I wear?"

"Whichever one you want, if you'd like I will send someone up to help you get ready"

"Oh, yes please. That will help me out a lot. I'm just so new to this; I'm scared I will mess something up"

"Nonsense, you're a princess now, and princesses never mess up. Everyone else does."

"Wait, I'm a what? Could you say that again for me real fast?"

"You're simply a princess. Nothing extreme"

"Did you seriously just say nothing extreme? Do you hear yourself right now? You sound so crazy it's not even funny." I said trying my best to hold back a giggle. Was this guy for real?

"Yes, I seriously just said nothing extreme. No I'm not crazy and what I am saying are the facts . . . whether you like it or not"

"Fine then goes send someone up to help me. And I will go wash up right now"

"Alright, give me a few minutes and someone will be up to help you"

CHAPTER 11

I turned around and walked back into my room. Wait, there is no bathroom. I looked around and I still didn't see a door that led to a bathroom, maybe there was some kind of secret door or something. That when I saw it, a small door on the other side of the bed. I walked over and turned the knob and opened the door.

As soon as I opened it I saw a beautiful bathtub that could easily fit five. A sink that was the size of two regular sized kitchen sinks. A mirror with gold trimming that was the size of an entire wall. A beautiful diamond and gold chandelier hung from the ceiling. There was what looked like another door, so I walked over to it and opened it up. I peeked around the corner to see what was in there. I froze with amazement; there was a mini waterfall with a pool of water at the bottom of it. This must be used as a shower.

I decided that I would take a shower before I got dresses for dinner. Mostly . . . because it looked so awesome. I left the bathroom and went to the dresser to look for a bathrobe. But all I could find in the dresser were corsets, stockings, and undergarments. So I shut the drawers and walked over to the closet and as I was about to open the doors, there was a knock on my door.

When I opened the door I saw a young girl about my age, she has big emerald green eyes, rose pink lips, fair skin and freckles seemed to dust her nose and cheeks. She wore a silver gown with gold lace around the arms, torso and bottom of the dress. She had long blonde hair pulled back into what looked like an extremely formal bun. That when I noticed she was wearing a crown, a little bit smaller than the smallest one in the closet.

"Hello, my name is Mackenzie but people call me Max. I'd like you to call me Max as well. It's a pleasure to meet you; I didn't think there were other girls here around my age"

"The pleasure is mine, and there are but a few girls our age about the castle"

"Oh okay, so what's your name?"

"My apologies, I seem to have forgotten to introduce myself. My name is Natalya"

"Oh that's pretty"

"Thank you" she said and curtsied.

"I noticed that you're wearing a crown . . . are you part of a royal family or something?"

"My father doesn't like for me to talk about it, but yes I am. I am not the true heir to the throne of course, my sister is. Although I have yet to meet her, however father says that she will join us shortly"

I don't even know why I am talking to some commoner that just happened to get lucky and made a princess. She might be a princess now, but to me she is still a filthy commoner. I do not care whether dad wants her here or not. I don't. If I have to I am going to do everything in my power to make sure she does not even touch the throne. I might not be the rightful heir but I'm still in line for it! And I do not care how man commoner's father throws at me; it's going to be mine. Especially in two months when it is my birthday. Because that's when I become the legal age to assume the throne! And that it that.

"That's very interesting" she said smiling.

"Yes it is, I can't wait to meet her. I just know that she will be perfect"

"Wow, they take the throne thing seriously around here" I thought to myself.

"Yes well I hope she don't disappoint, and I need help with getting ready for dinner, do you think-"

"Oh, of course, I would be delighted to help you" she said with a smile on her face.

"Why don't you come in?" I said as I moved aside for her to enter the room.

"You know, I've always loved this room. I and my mother used to play in here when I was a child"

"Oh, well that's sweet . . . so um the closets over there. Do you think will have enough time to take a shower before dinner?" I asked her.

"Oh yes, of course you will, dinner won't be ready for about two hours any how"

"It takes that long to make dinner?"

"No, usually it takes a little over four hours, but father has extra people on duty so the food will be prepared faster"

"Wow . . . so why exactly does it take that long?"

"Well we have Martha, the cook, run to the market and pick up eggs, turkey, chicken, ham vegetables and spices. But before she leaves, Tyler has to hook the horse up to the cart, and put the saddle on him. The she goes to town which usually takes about thirty minutes, then she has to pick out everything she needs separately, we also give her money to buy food for her children. Then when she is done shopping she has to put all the food into the cart and then mount the horse and ride back which takes longer than thirty minutes or so. From there she has to pack everything into the kitchen . . . where the kitchen staff and she cleans and prepares the food. It takes an unfortunately long time, but when they are finished the food is delicious"

"I bet it is. So what color do you think will look best on me?"

"Red, definitely red, after dinner if you wish I will have someone come up and replace all the gowns with red ones. That is while we're eating dinner. The servants aren't allowed to enter the bed rooms while the guest or residents are in them."

"Oh okay . . . and yes that would be nice. Thank you"

"No problem, now let's get your dress picked out. And then get you into the bath."

"Alright"

As she was trying to find me a dress I couldn't help but notice that she has the exact same necklace as I do. It was the exact same shape, style as well as the exact same size. It was odd how when I first got here I didn't know what was going on and now suddenly I'm a princess. I mean I don't even miss home. Oh my god, home . . . mom is going to freak if I don't get back soon. Then again she shouldn't have been lying to me all these years, even if it was to protect me.

After what seemed like ages she found the "right" dress. It was exhausting to realize how much work it takes to be a princess. And that's just to pick out the right dress. I would've thought that any of them would be the right one, but I guess not. I snapped out of my thoughts when she started reaching for a crown.

"What are you doing? They aren't yours, I'm not even sure if they're mine"

"Trust me; father wouldn't have given you this room if he didn't want you to enjoy everything in it."

"I guess you could be right. Okay so when can I take a bath?"

"We're going there now. Can you grab the robe that's on the hanger, right there please?"

"Sure thing"

"We'll work on you being a bit more proper in your word choices later, but as of right now we need to get you washed up for dinner?"

"Oh . . . alright"

"You need to go and get into the bath for right now, I will bring you your soap and shampoo momentarily . . . alright?"

"Okay, gladly" I said feeling kind of stupid.

"Anything else?" she asked with a big smile on her face.

"Uh yeah . . . where did you get that necklace? I have the exact same one, see?" I said as I was trying to take the necklace off to show her. I couldn't believe I was about to take it off, but I did anyway.

"How interesting, only members of the royal family have these. Surely you found it somewhere?"

"No, actually I didn't, I've had it for as long as I can remember . . . I've never taken it off, until now." I replied in a bit of shock.

"Oh well I guess its coincidence then"

I couldn't believe what I was seeing . . . she wears an amulet only royals have. Surely she was lying, she has to be. Only the *royal* family has them, she cannot be a royal. Well even if she wasn't lying she still needs a lot of work. She doesn't know anything about being royalty, *obviously.*

"I guess so . . . imma go get in the tub, can you try and hurry with my stuff?"

"Yes, I will try and hurry with your *stuff*"

"Thanks"

"Yes well, you're very welcome"

She is such an imbecile, she knows nothing and if she is to be a princess then she needs to get rid of that vocabulary . . . it is very unladylike. She is starting to aggravate me now; I just hope that I don't have to spend any more time with her after this. Father owes me . . . . big time.

CHAPTER 12

This girl is super weird. She talks, walks and dresses like the girls in movies do. I don't know if it's just because I'm not used to it or . . . yea she's weird. I wonder if I have to talk like that now, hopefully not.

I was still thinking about what I'd be like if I had to live like Natalya, when I got into the shower. A few minutes later she brought me something that I supposed, was used for soap. And when I was done with that she gave me a jar of what resembled lotion. It was very odd. When I got out of the shower I asked if she had anything I could brush my teeth with and she brought me back, *fresh* twig's and chalk. Talk about a bad day, first I have to use lotion for shampoo, now she expects me to brush my teeth with twig's and chalk . . . . what kind of place was this?

"Ok so I'm done", I said as I was walking out of the bathroom.

"Alright, now we need to get you dressed. Could you come over here a moment and step on this for me?"

"Step on what exactly? There's nothing there."

"Oh, but there is." She said smiling as she conjured up what I think was supposed to be a stool.

"Wow, that's pretty cool. How'd you do that? Can you teach me?"

"It is called training, and no I don't think I could. It took me a few weeks just to get this spell right. I suppose you will need to take lessons as well."

"You're probably right, so when can I start these lessons?" I said excited, if I can take lessons then I will learn how to do even more stuff then I can now, which isn't very much.

"You may be enrolled in lessons, as soon as you get permission from my father of course. But all of that however depends on how long you will be here, and if you're ready"

"Oh okay, so what are we going to do now?"

"Why we are going to get you dressed of course. Sylvia you may come in now, I need your help with getting Miss Mackenzie ready for dinner"

"Yes madam"

"Sylvia, would you be so kind, as to help me get Miss Mackenzie ready?" She asked in a stern voice.

"Of course, it would be my pleasure. Miss Mackenzie, would you step onto the stool for me please?" she asked in a sheepish tone.

"Of course I ill, so what exactly are we going to do?" I asked

"Well first we need to get you into some stockings and a corset then we will go from there." She said very determined.

"Wait, corset . . . stockings? I've never worn either, are they uncomfortable?"

"No madam, they are not, they are actually kind of pleasant" said Sylvia.

"Alright, I will put them on"

She was right, stockings aren't uncomfortable at all. But the corset is the one that I'm really concerned about. I was trying to keep my balance as she was lacing the corset but it wasn't easy will all the pulling and fastening. Once it was on it wasn't as bad though.

"Okay Miss Mackenzie your corset is completely finished. Now we need to get you into your dress"

"Okay" I said a little bit worried.

Chapter 13

After the corset I thought she was just going to put the dress on me but I was wrong. She got a something that looked like a long round wired skirt, from the closet. She put that around me and fastened all the clamps that went down the back. It felt like it weighed about ten pounds. After that was done, she went back to the closet and got out a big white layered skirt that went over the wired one. I was exhausted at this point but, unfortunately I was far from done. When she went over to the closet a third time she brought out the medium sized crown and sat it down on the dresser. After what seemed like hours I was finally in my dress. Unfortunately she had a lot of touchups that she had to do. Then it was time for the hair . . . oh no, I'm in trouble now. Sylvia brushed my hair a few times, and then she combed it. She had out all kinds of bobby-pins and ribbons that she was going to but in my hair. She kept twisting, braiding, brushing and curling my hair until she smiled and said "I'm finished."

As I turned around a mirror appeared but I didn't realize who I was looking at until I really looked. It was me, and I was . . . . I was beautiful. I had ribbons braided into my hair that was going back into what I considered a bun. There was something that looked like a hair net with pearls on it, on my bun. The crown she got out was placed perfectly on top of my head. I couldn't help but feel overwhelmed at that moment. But that wasn't all; I was wearing a dress that looked like it had come from a movie. It was a beautiful deep red, with sleeves that only covered my shoulders. From the waist down the dress was split, and pulled back over the 'underskirt' as Sylvia called it. The dress had amazing detailing. The torso had jewels and pearls that were arranged in beautiful designs. The place that was split as well as my sleeves had gold trimming. I couldn't help but feel like a serious princess.

"You look beautiful" Natalya said with a slight smile on her face.

"Ok, good. I'm starving are we going to go eat now or what?" I asked kind of hungry.

"Yes we are going to eat now . . . will you kindly follow me? And don't ask a lot of questions on our way there" said Natalya sounding kind of agitated.

We walked down the long hallway that my room was on, down a flight of stairs. Then we turned left and went down another long hallway. After all that we were finally there. At this point I felt like the dress weighed more than me. When we walked up to the door the guards opened them and then the Harold announced our arrival and said our names. I heard a lot of clapping only to realize I had to walk down to more flights of stairs, they weren't as long as the last one but seriously? How many flights of stair cases does this place have?

"My dear daughter, Mackenzie-" the man started to say; only to be interrupted by none other than . . . Natalya.

"Did you just say daughter?" no way! She is not your daughter, and certainly not my sister! She can't be, she's to . . . she is too stupid to be a princess let alone a queen!"

"Natalya, I suggest you hold your tongue." He said in an extremely strict and stern voice.

"NO! I can't believe you're doing this to me! First mom died and now I have to put up with some moron, whom you expect *me* to accept as my sister!"

"You will do as I say! I told you to hold your tongue and I suggest you do that now! Do you understand me?"

"No I don't . . . all I'm hearing from you is-"

"Natalya. Why do you speak to your own father in that tone?" said some guy I didn't know; well not yet anyway.

"None of your business, I can talk to whoever I want the way I want . . . that's what a princess doe-" she was saying and as she spun around she froze. My guess was that she knew this guy and that she was embarrassed. Yup she was embarrassed.

"Oh, prince Zachariah, hello . . . lovely night isn't it? Besides it being cold out" she said in a sheepish voice.

"Yes, well I would rather be out there for the rest of the evening than be in hear listening to you disobey and shame your father in front of all these people . . . come with me please" Zachariah said.

"Sure . . . will you all excuse me a moment" she asked just barley loud enough for everyone to hear. As she exited the room, everyone started whispering, and talking. My guess was that they were talking about the incident that had just occurred.

How could she embarrass me like that? I can't believe it . . . she actually made me mad. Man I have got to get a grip; I can't let little brats make me look bad. It just doesn't work like that. And on top of all of that she embarrassed me in front of Zachariah; if I am supposed to marry him I can't be letting people like her get in the way. We walked until we came upon the doors to the library; this isn't going to be good. People only go into the library to argue, that's what it's always been used for around here. It's big and extremely quiet and no one's ever in there. Plus there are books to throw. That's what makes it the perfect place to have an argument/discussion.

"How dare you embarrass your father like that? I cannot believe you, you have never disrespected anyone" Zachariah said, his face turning red in the process.

"I am sorry, I did not mean to"

"Just like you did not mean to come here tonight, right? No . . . you did mean to and you will apologize when you go back in there. Do you understand me?"

"Yes but-"

"No buts, you made a mistake and now you will accept the consequences"

"Mistake . . . mistake! I did not make a mistake, how dare she come in here, and take away . . . everything that I am. I'm supposed to take the throne not her!" I said pointing to the door and trying my best to hold back tears.

"How can she take away everything that you are if you're so much more than any throne or crown?"

"What else am I then? Can you tell me that . . . I don't think you can, how can you? I can't even answer that myself"

"You are more exquisite and beautiful than any rose in Hera's eternal garden"

"Do you really think so?" I asked as tears started pouring down my cheeks like someone had just poured a bucket of water over my head.

"I know so, why are you crying? Please don't cry, it rips my heart seeing you like this. Please don't"

"I have absolutely no idea why I'm crying. I don't even know what emotion I'm feeling right now"

"It happens to the best of us"

CHAPTER 14

How could she do this to her own father? Humiliate him, and treat him like pig scrap, as if he is nothing? She has shamed her whole family . . . . she's shamed me. If I were to marry her now as our parents had planned then my kingdom should be shamed as well. You just cannot marry someone who has humiliated and degraded their entire family, for that brings shame to that family as well.

But her sister however has not. Not to mention that her beauty is very striking, she would make an excellent queen . . . . my queen. If I only knew her magic level, for if she has powerful magic that would make her eligible for marriage to another throne. Natalya is aware of that however, so I fear she will try to sabotage her exams. Hmm, I will just have to make sure she does not get the opportunity to do so. Now what was her name? Marie? No that's not it, ah Mackenzie, of course, and what a splendid name for a queen.

"My dearest Natalya, would you be so kind, as to give me to greatest honor as to escort you to King Richardson's ball in a fort night?"

"Yes, however Mackenzie's exams begin at that time. I fear she would think even less of me, not because of how I treated her but because I would be absent of such an important event in her life"

"So then you will leave me to go alone and curse me with that of temporary loneliness because you are scared of what some peasant will think of you?"

"Of course not, as if I could ever burden you with that horrible and retched emotion. I would be delighted to accompany such a gallant man to the ball."

"That is the most joyful of news my lady, we shall head back to the dinner."

"Yes, of course my prince, they are likely to miss us before long"

As we walked back to the dining hall I couldn't help but think about Mackenzie, and how beautiful she was. My word, she would make an amazing queen. If only I could get close enough to her heart to announce my proposal. I mean after all she can decline, if she feels she needs to. Which in that case I can just use an enchantment, so either way it shall work out fine; I will do whatever it takes to not have to marry Natalya.

When Natalya and Zachariah walked back into the dining hall, she looked like the happiest person on the planet. He however looked like the most miserable person I have ever seen. I couldn't help but wonder what had happened while they were gone. Natalya whispered something into the Harold's ear and then he announced their re-arrival. Just then Natalya stepped forward and put her hands on the balcony beside where I stood. She turned to me then turned back toward the large group of people watching closely. I wondered who all these people were . . . the only ones I knew were Dad, Natalya, Zachariah, and Sylvia. This was it . . . Natalya started to speak.

"Friends, family, Father, I am very sorry for what I have said I am forever ashamed of how I reacted . . . I hope you all accept my apologies. Mackenzie, my dear sister, I am also sorry for how I have treated you tonight, and I would understand if you do not accept my apology to you. For I have ashamed and embarrassed you and your honor."

The air was thick with tension and I didn't know what to say. Should I honestly forgive her for doing that to me? Well if I'm going to be a good sister and princess I'm going to need all the practice I can get. And honestly I wouldn't mind having a little sister; I have always wanted one.

"Yes, Natalya I forgive you . . . , you know I have always wanted a little sister, just didn't know I already had one." Then the crowd started to chuckle it was kind of weird for a moment. Then I heard cheering and applause, that's when I realized she was hugging me, but I wasn't hugging back. I decided to change that. We embarrassed each other for a moment then we turned to the audience and smiled brightly.

Chapter 15

I was so proud of my daughter, putting their differences aside and making the best of what they had. I also need to thank Zachariah for coming Natalya down, or that would have been a bigger mess than it already was.

"My dear daughters . . . I am so glad that you have put your differences aside. Mackenzie, my dear, I need to speak to you a moment before we all sit down to eat this beautiful feast our generous kitchen staff has prepared for us."

"Yes, shall we leave know Father?" she said.

"Yes my dear, that would be splendid . . . will you please follow me?"

We walked for a while before we entered the throne room. I had something I wanted her to see.

"Mackenzie my dear, you are aware of the story of your mother right? How she was a queen and a beloved mother?"

"No, I have not yet been told anything about her"

"Well my dear, she had the bravest heart of any women I have ever met. She cared for everyone, went to the village three days a week, to give out money to the less fortunate and buy bread for the homeless. She was a beloved queen by everyone; when she died the kingdom almost fell apart. Natalya helped me stay strong, and helped me put the kingdom back together, so to speak. That is why she is mostly offended by your arrival."

"I didn't mean to hurt anyone, or cause any trouble."

"You have not caused any trouble my dear. It is okay"

"Are you sure?"

"Yes I am very sure my dear; I must tell you that you are the rightful heir to the throne."

"Why me?"

"Because, you were the first queen's daughter"

The first queen, I thought she lived thousands of years ago"

"She did"

"So how am I her daughter?"

"The prophecy says, that before she was murdered she put all of her magic into an egg, formed the egg to protect it with magic, as to be specific, a magical amulet"

"And"

"And my dear, you wear that amulet around your neck at this very moment"

"That's not true; I am not thousands of years old!"

"You were created thousands of years ago, as I said; you were hatched from an egg"

"This does not make sense I am not a bird"

"No my dear you are not, you are however the first queen's daughter"

"Ok fine, so I accept being the first queen's daughter, now what?"

"Now I must tell you about exams you must take to assure that you're taking the throne. Passing the exams is also very important, for if you fail you are not allowed to marry."

"So I need to pass an exam to assure the throne and to get married?"

"Exactly"

"Alright, what is the test consists of, and what are they for?"

"The exams are given to see how powerful your magic is."

"Magic . . . I have not learned how to control; it so will I ever pass?"

"For a natural heir it is usually simpler and a lot easier than for the others. I will assign you a teacher as well as a tutor that will teach you how to control it."

"Ok, so who is my teacher and who will be my tutor?"

"Have you ever heard of Ancients?"

"No sir."

"Then let me inform you of exactly who they are."

"Okay I am listening."

"The Ancients are a group of magicians that are almost as old as Vitoria itself."

"Wow that's really old huh?"

"Yes dear, an ancient always teaches the first born in every generation, for our family and that is you." "Wow that must be some honor then"

"Yes it actually is a great honor."

"So is another ancient going to tutor me?"

"No Prince Zachariah will"

"Ok so what kind of exams are they exactly?"

"There are five exams or as you say test. In the first test an ancient will determine what your skill level is. In the second one you will face three mini tests that will involve you using your magic to survive. In the third test you will face an opponent that the ancients randomly chose for you. In the fourth you will face another opponent that will be twice as strong as the first one. In the fifth and final test you will face many opponents all at once and you will need to defeat them all in order to pass the test."

"This is quite a bit of work is it not?"

"Yes dear, it is"

"How long do these exams last?"

"With no interruptions it takes around two weeks."

"How long will I have to train?"

"Little under one week"

"So let me get all of this straight, I am expected to learn how to use and control my magic in 6 days and learn how to defeat the exams?"

"Yes"

"How will this work?"

"It just wills, the exams have been happening the same way for thousands of generations"

"I do not know if I can do it"

"What does that mean?"

"It means I am not sure if I will be able to handle this."

"You must never dought yourself, my dear."

"When do I start training?"

"In three days."

"Three days? That soon, what if I am not ready?"

"You are a Delemorte of course you will be ready"

"I hope your right."

Chapter 16

I could not believe what I was hearing. How could he be expect me to train for a week to take the exams that are going to last two weeks? This is obscured; yes that is what it is obscured. No way am I going to be able to do all of this . . . . No way at all.

"Alright if you think so then, I think I can too"

Okay so let's get back to the dining room where the others are waiting."

"Alright, who are all of those people anyway?"

"They are mostly friends, some family and the warriors came tonight as well."

"Warrior's, that's kind of scary, what do they do exactly?"

"Well they will train to be masters in the battle."

"I could tell that they battle, it's what a warrior is what kind of battle?"

"They battle horrific creatures that get loose, invade or threaten kingdoms,"

"So then whenever there's like a dragon or some other creature like that on the loose they chase it down and fight it?"

"Yes"

"Wow, that's so awesome, so were you ever a warrior?"

"No, but me and their principles, went to school together and we'd always get together after school."

"Who's their principle, is he a warrior too?"

"Yes he's a warrior and his name is Christopher. Actually I think he's here with them."

"Wow that's amazing, Can I meet the warrior's and Christopher?"

"Yes I'm sure you can if we leave now we might be able to catch them before dinner?"

"Why before dinner?"

"Because they don't usually stay unless they are invited"

"So why are they here then?"

"To see you of course"

"Why do they want to see me?"

"How can they protect a princess if they don't know what she looks like?"

"Good point . . . so why won't you invite them?"

"I guess I've never really thought about it . . . would you like me to make sure they stay?"

"Will you do that for me?"

"Of course"

"That's amazing. I can't wait to hear all about the monsters that they face.

"If it really fascinates you that much, I will have a warrior tutor you."

"What about Zachariah?"

"Well I was going to have him teach you the basics battles methods anyway."

"Ok . . . Let's get going then."

"Okay"

What's taking them so long? I just apologized and now they've abandoned me. Oh my gosh this really isn't fair, but I have to be nice if I'm going to get close to Zachariah. Wait if dad chooses him to tutor her then he won't be able to take me to that ball. I have to do something about this.

"Zach, can I ask you something real fast?"

"You know it's not polite to talk while the king is away."

"I know but it will only take a second."

"Alright what it is it?"

"If dad chooses you to tutor Mackenzie will you still be able to take me to the ball?"

"I will make sure that I have enough time there is nothing I would rather do except take you to the ball."

"You're so sweet"

"Yes my dear, but you're even more breath-taking than the biggest, brightest, most colorful rose in all the worlds."

"That's so sweet of you to say."

"I am so glad you think so, because I feel that I have offended your beauty with something so cheap."

"No never"

"You have lifted the biggest, heaviest burden I have ever faced right off my shoulders."

"I am glad I was able to help."

CHAPTER 17

My word this girl is naïve. If only she knew that I was just using her to get to her sister. Yes, that does seem kind of selfish, but I only speak the truth.

"Yes you have helped me more than you anyone ever could."

"I am so glad you feel this way."

"You're happy, I feel like the happiest, man in the world every time I hear a word come from your lips."

"Wow that's so sweet of you to say . . . dad is coming."

"Yes indeed he is. Would you like to join me greeting them back?"

"Yes I would love that."

"Good"

As the king and Mackenzie walk through the door, Natalya approached them and says "my dear dad, my most grateful sister, welcome back, I feel as if happiness was washed over the room again."

"My dear sweet Natalya I am glad you feel that way because I have an announcement to make" the king said to her smiling.

Here it comes; he is going to announce that I am to tutor Mackenzie in her lessons on battle. I have been waiting for this moment ever since it was announced that the rightful heir had returned.

"Dear friends, family, I would like to announce that senior Warrior Aaron will be tutoring my daughter princess Mackenzie in her battle lessons"

"My king surely there is someone more suitable and qualified to have such an honor. I propose that someone her age may be more likely to connect with the princess and it would be easier to teach her based on that connection"

"Yes, I suppose you may be right, she shall be taught in the ways of magic by two ancients as well as two seniors and the highest qualified students of the enchanted arts high school for scholars"

"My king that has been done but once"

"Yes, it was done for the first queen the divine Queen Mariana, may her soul rest in peace. Listen, for I say it first. My daughter will be one of great power and her name shall go into the great book of records right beside our great queen."

"Surely you don't think that she is of such power you surely know you must be exaggerating"

"How dare you come into my house and not only doubt my judgment but question my daughter's abilities!"

"No sir, I do no such thing. I am speaking for the sake of your daughter. I say not that she does not deserve the very best of everything but that if you give her more than she does deserve are you but setting her up for humiliation?"

"I will hold exams in one fortnight exact; all who desire to observe what power my daughter possesses shall come to the arena to witness a miraculous event that will go down in history!"

"Yes sir"

"Father, I don't think that Prince Zachariah meant any harm or disgrace to you or our family, I presume he wanted what was best for my darling sister, *and* you're first born daughter" stated Natalya.

"I presume you could be right. She will have two tutors"

"Two? Why of course. Splendid idea my king"

"My dear friends and family, I have yet another announcement; and if anyone thinks I am but wrong then step forth and present your case, and tell me why you question my decision for my first born child"

CHAPTER 18

W hen no one stepped forth I knew that everyone was in too much shock to say anything. I couldn't believe what I was hearing; my dad was giving me *two* tutors? That can't be good. I don't know what it means but the looks on everyone's faces and how unhappy Zachariah was; it couldn't be even remotely good.

"Are you sure you want to do this?" I finally stepped forth and asked him.

"Yes I am, you are my first born daughter and I know you have a lot of power and maybe more than we can comprehend"

"Are you sure? This is all new to me so I am kind of confused, but this can't be right"

"I know it is, I've lost you once and now that I have an opportunity to make it up to you, I only want what's best for you and nothing less"

"Thank you father, but I'm not sure if I can handle two tutors heck, I'm not sure I can even handle one"

"Well I am most positive that you shall succeed at any task you are given and surpass any expectation they set for you"

"Okay, well if you are that sure I guess I will give it my best effort"

"That is all I ask"

"Okay so who is my other tutor?"

"Senior warrior Damian"

"Okay, now I'm starving so let's go eat"

"As you wish, and now we feast!" He said loudly turning to the group of people.

CHAPTER 19

The rest of the night went without any disturbances. I had already met prince Zachariah. Later that night I met the warriors who were going to tutor me in my battle classes. They were very nice and exceedingly smart as well. The first one I met was Aaron. He had shaggy dark brown hair, sky blue eyes, pale pink lips and cheeks; he was tan and talked in such a manly voice it was kind of scary. My other tutor, whose name was Damian, I met next. He had shaggy sandy blonde hair, bright emerald green eyes that had specks of gold, alabaster skin, a perfect smile, and had a manly voice but with a British accent. They both wore blue jeans and black t-shits, the kind that stuck to your skin which complimented their muscles very well.

After the dinner I went back to my room, I had to have Sylvia help me get out of my dress, and then find me some pajamas. After about thirty minutes, and endless pairs of pajamas, I finally decided to go with the silky maroon pants, and button down top. We went through a few drawers and about twenty shoe boxes before we found any house shoes, but they were fluffy and white and felt amazing on my feet after being in high heels all day. Finally I was able to go to sleep, and I welcomed it openly.

CHAPTER 20

At first I thought I was alone, but when my eyes adjusted to the dark light around me, I realized that there were people marching around me, that were all in black hooded cloaks. I couldn't see any of their faces because they all had strange wooden masks on that was shaped like a type of exotic bird. I was strapped to what I thought was a stone table of some sort. There were metal straps around my hands and feet, I had something tied tight over my mouth so I couldn't scream. Then, they all stopped in place, and another person who was wearing; a long white rope and a huge bird mask with a lot of feathers sticking out approached me. I was still strapped to the table, I normally would have already been able to break them, but these straps were enforced with a type of magic that weakened me. The person in the white rope pulled out a dagger, started chanting in a foreign language, cut off whatever was tied over my mouth, I started to panic. He then proceeded to drag the dragger down to my forearms, then down to my thighs, and shins. I screamed as loud as I could, hoping someone would hear me but no one came. He stopped cutting me, and started chanting once again. One of the other bird—people brought him long golden needles, which he stabbed into the beginning and end of each cut; both my arms were covered in blood, as well as my legs. When I thought it was over, he pulled the dagger out again and started to carve the crescent moon and star into my stomach. I was in so much pain, I couldn't help but cry. When I thought he was done, he used magic to burn my skin where the crescent moon and star was. The image was forever burned onto my skin. As blackness swept over me, I heard screaming and the sound of flesh being cut.

When I woke up, I was no longer in my bed; I was on the bathroom floor. I had no idea how I got there, but I did know I was in a lot of pain. When I looked down I realized that my shirt was covered in blood, I pulled my shirt up far enough to confirm my fears, the image from my dream was carved and burnt into my skin. At that moment I was extremely weak, but I still had enough strength to scream as loud as I could and just hope that someone heard me.

I and Natalya were at the breakfast table eating when we both heard screaming.

"Natalya, is Mackenzie up yet?"

"When I went by to wake her up she was asleep. She looked so peaceful; I didn't want to wake her up. So I don't think she is."

"Ok come with me please, and hurry . . . it's a good thing you're not wearing one of them outrageous dresses of yours"

"I know"

We were down the hall from Mackenzie's room when the screaming stopped. Something was very wrong; I could feel it in every bone in my body. When we got to Max's house she wasn't in her bed, so I ran into the bathroom. As I burst in the door I seen her lying on the floor, her shirt was raise up enough for me to see the burn . . . a burn exactly like her mother's. But how could see do something like this? And for it to be exactly like Mariana's, something was wrong.

"Natalya get some help, and hurry" I yelled at her trying to hold back tears.

She looked so scared but she went anyways. I really hope'd this hadn't happened to her, something must be wrong with the prophecies, this happened to her mother and now her. This cannot be a coincident, there's no way it can be.

I just hope I got here in time to save her life like I had her mother.

CHAPTER 21

As we ran into her bathroom I'd seen her on the floor in blood, there was so much blood. She can't die I just got her, now she's going to be taken away from me. I may not exactly like her but I don't hate her.

As dad yelled for me to go I was terrified that he knew she was dead. I prayed that she was still alive all the way down to the kitchen.

"Mia, go get a doctor now, it's Mackenzie. She's hurt bad, and has lost a lot of blood. Tell the doctor that she's the lost heir and it's an emergency." I started to leave the room when I turned around.

"And tell him to bring a healer, she's lost a lot of blood and has serious burns . . . now go" I yelled.

"Yes ma'am, I will" she said as she scurried out the door. I looked out the window and I seen her pass by the window extremely fast, I couldn't tell but I think she was riding bare back. I never even knew she could ride.

I ran out of the kitchen down the hall and up the stairs back to Mackenzie's room. As I reentered the bathroom I saw dad on his knees with Max's body laid across his lab. He was crying, I never seen him cry before, it was almost scary. She was still bleeding I knew because there was more blood than before. She had a lot of cuts, down her arms . . .

"Dad . . . What happened, did u cut her?"

He looked at me with eyes filled with sorrow and misery "no . . . I did not cut her, she cut herself" h said in a small, weak voice.

"But she's not even awake, how could she cut herself?"

"Because the burn happened in her dream, when she tried to heal the burn it activated the rest of the pain inflicted upon her in her dream, which means the cuts appeared shortly after"

"But she's not a healer"

"Yes she is, she has that ability"

"How"

"I will explain it to you both when she wakes up"

"Ok but for now, something is wrong, she is still bleeding, her arms are bandaged that must be."

"What must it mean?"

"Her legs OH MY GOD . . . they are bleeding to, come on we have to get them wrapped up to, where are some scissors?"

"In the cabinet, over there hurry up . . . wait why do we need scissors?"

"We have to cut her pants; if her legs are really bleeding then we need to get them wrapped up as well"

"Hurry up though, and please don't cut her. If I'm right her legs are worst then her arms"

"Can I ask you something?"

"Anything but hurry up and be careful"

"I will, and is this how mom got all of her scars?"

"What . . . did you just say?"

"Her scars, is this how mom got hr scars?"

"How'd you know about them? She never showed anyone . . . who told you about that?"

"No one, I just. I was curious so I snooped around the doctor's reports, and I read a file that said she had multiple cuts, and that she would most likely have scars . . . there were pictures in the folder, pictures of her scars. But why do they match Mackenzie's?"

"Because the exact same thing is happening to Mackenzie as it did your mother. She was taunted by dreams of a clan cutting her and chanting."

"Chanting what exactly?"

"We didn't know it was all in Greek. We just never figured out what the words were."

CHAPTER 22

The dream kept replaying in my head, even after I lost conciseness. When I woke I was in my bedroom, I looked over to my right and the bathroom door was open, there was blood, and lots of it. Blood was everywhere and my pajamas were on the floor," Oh my God, Please don't let me be naked" was all I could think. As I started to move my whole body hurt, and stung. But I didn't care, I rose up the covers, and was instantly relieved, I was in a night gown. When I turned to my left, I saw dad . . . wait what was dad doing here? He looked so panicked, afraid, and I could tell he'd been crying. Like all guys do when they cry, his eyes were red and puffy; he was sniffling and looking down to the ground.

"Dad . . . what are you doing her and what-"

"Hello dear sister, how are feeling?" Natalya said instantly.

"You don't remember?"

"No I don't as I turned around and faced the bathroom door and said in a whisper

"You wouldn't believe me anyway"

"Oh well don't worry about it I-"

The exact same thing that happened to you happened to mom. Dad was scared he didn't get to you in time to save your life, did I mention he saved mom's life when this happened to her. How awesome is that? I bet it's like some kind of curse or something." Natalya said, I couldn't help but notice that she sound kind of excited.

"It happened to my mom too? Where was she when it happens? How old was she? What did she do afterward? I asked turning to face dad.

"It was a long time ago" he said in a small voice

"Tell us, from the beginning"

"Ok . . . it was around the time she started her exams, two days before, to be exact. One night while we were training, I had left her in the room to go get us a drink, when I return there were people in the hoods were coming up behind her. I yelled at her told her to watch out; she accessed her power faster than anyone I had ever seen. We fought them together, we fought them for hours, and every time we killed them they would come back. When we decapitated them, their head reattached to their body. We made a pack, we would continue to fight as long as we could, and we would not surrender and if we failed to kill them for good, she was surrender and let them take her while I still fought. In the end, we failed. They took her and vanished, but they didn't know that she had cast a spell to make our bond stronger."

"Wait, what's a bond?"

"I'll explain that when I'm done"

"Ok continue"

"As I was saying, she had cast a spell to make our bond stronger, so I could find her where ever she went. I followed them for days before we came upon a sanctuary swarming with birds and that; they had made her unconscious so she could not fight back. I fought my way into the sanctuary, as I came through the doors, I felt every cut they made, every needle that went through her, and it was like it was happening to me. I felt her dying with every drop of blood that left her body. I fought through the pain, and found her right as they were about to sacrifice her. I slammed open the doors as I felt her fade into unconsciousness. I fought away all the bird people, killed every one of them. I didn't know how I did, but every time I sliced it was like they weakened. I finished off the bird-people right as she was on the edge of death. I was feeding her my power."

"What do you mean you were feeding her your power?"

"I will explain that too, when I'm done"

"Ok"

"As I was saying, I feed her my powers until she was able to heal herself. When she was woken, I was right there beside her, I kissed her gently on the fore head and pick her up and carried her back to the castle. The following year, when she was well enough, she took her examines. She passed, and we got married. Then Sicilia, came into our lives, she got close to your mother as betrayed her. We were expecting a child, a little girl. And somehow she knew either would survive, unless she was able to use her magic to move the baby to a safer place, the egg. She practiced for months, when she finally thought she was able to do it, Sicilia came for her. She ran through the castle and tried her best to dodge every spell Sicilia cast at her. She made it to her room, when she was safe enough to start the spell she did. She used her magic; first to create the egg so the baby would have somewhere to stay until it was strong enough to live on its own, then she used her magic to transport her into the egg. She knew it was our child wouldn't be able to live without protection, even if she didn't remain inside the egg. She took off her amulet and wrapped it around the egg; cast a spell to insure it would remain forever safe. Only the purest of hearts and intentions were able to pick up the egg and not be burnt or killed. When Sicilia got into the room, and saw Mariana was not wearing her amulet she killed her, since she knew the child would be a problem she tried to kill it to, but the amulet burned her skin so bad it almost killed her. She knew the child could only be killed when it removed the necklace so she remained until it hatched, when it hatched and she saw the child, the child looked like Mariana, her regret and grieve took over and she couldn't kill it. But over the years she regained her strength and cruelty and decided the day the amulet was removed she would strike . . . that's the end"

"How do you know all of this?"

"I and queen Mariana were bonded, we shared the same soul. Which means I could access everything that was happening to her every time, it also means whatever she felt I felt, whatever happened to her, and in a way happened to me"

"Wow that's so romantic but also very freaky, ok so what do you mean by you was feeding her your powers?" Natalya said excitedly

"What I meant was I was giving her my power by forcing it through the bond. She had to expect it, she did, and she was able to heal herself because of it"

"Wow, that's so awesome!" I said, and then asked "How do you make a bond?"

"A bond in a way is made when soul's match is created. Which mean the souls are linked, when the two souls's come in contact they bond, and the bond grows stronger with every emotion you sure, every touch, every word? Our bond was the strongest ever made, and when she died, I died to. I felt empty, like I was alone and almost went crazy"

"That's sad, so what fixed you?"

"Our little girl hatched, and when I held her, my life was restored, I was happy again. Our little girl gave me hope that things would get better. And they did, until the day she was taken from me. Ever since I spent almost every day looking for her, I would have continued to do so if superiors didn't tell me I had to remarry and had another child. I went crazy, but all the villagers; I didn't kill anyone I just wanted to show my anger. The superiors didn't appreciate this and they told me that if I didn't listen to the orders they will find my daughter and kill her in front of me, I couldn't deal with that. So I obeyed their orders. That's when Natalya and her mother queen Natalie came into the picture."

"So you never loved my mom?" Natalya said sharply

"I loved your mom deeply!" he yelled

"But you only married her because you are following orders!" Natalya yelled back

"Yes but she also order to marry me! I loved your mother, not the way I loved Mariana but I still loved her more then you could image . . . she just liked Mariana, she was herself and that was more than enough for me! She was a great woman with a pure heart. When Mariana died I never thought there would be another person with such a pure heart, but then Natalie came into my life and I loved her ever since! I still do love her, so you will hold your tongue if you don't know facts!"

"Fine I am sorry" she said as she started to cry and walk out of the room.

"That was a bit harsh, and I am tired. I want to go to sleep" I said as I turned over to emphasize my point.

"Yes it was, I must now apologize to her, you get your rest my dear I will see you at dinner" he said then left the room.

CHAPTER 23

Later that night, we were all sitting around the table, when father began his story.

"The first queen of Nitoriah Queen Mariana was a prophet, and had many other unique abilities. Legend has it that the queen had nightmares only days before her murder. She woke with burns and scratches. She believed she was cursed, and that every queen that lived after her would suffer the same fate; dreams from which a queen would be tortured. As you both know, Queen Mariana put our children inside an egg. Babies born from magical beings drain their parents' power to help them survive; somehow the child knows when to stop taken the magic. But Queen Mariana's child which lived inside an egg would somehow drain the powers from one queen and one princess from every generation. People knew the egg was of poor heart parents, but thought egg was tainted by evil somehow during the process of being placed inside the egg. The ancients interfered and took the egg, examined it and decided that it was not evil. But they did however decide it was misjudged, that when Queen Mariana died the egg was confused and did not know how it should behave. The egg was like a child without a mother to teach it right from wrong; it only done what it knew how;

use magic to drain magic. They tried to teach it, but how do you teach something when you're not sure how to communicate with the child inside the egg? The day that it disappeared, the prophets believed that the egg was about to hatch knowing it was going to be safe with who ever had taken it"

"So you're saying that I have all the power in me; which I drained from others myself and that I probably killed people when I was a baby?"

"Yes, that's what exactly I am saying. And you didn't kill anyone; you just drained their powers, they survived, it was when you stopped taking their magic that they felt ill. It seems when you are draining their powers, you put a little of yours into them, which amped up their powers which made them stronger. And when you stopped their bodies were used to the powers, they needed it to survive. You stopped because, even as a child, you were afraid you would hurt them by taking too much. You were not aware of the opposite affect" dad said.

"Is that why you assigned me to ancients?"

"Yes it is, my dear you are the direct daughter of Queen Mariana the first queen of Nitoriah."

"No I never killed anyone?"

"No my dear, you did not"

"So do I have any other family? Like direct family from my mother?"

"As a matter of fact you have a cousin named Moon who's alive today; of course she doesn't live in this realm"

"Which realm does she live in? Wait realms as in realms? How many realms are there?"

"There are five magical realms. As well as five royal kingdoms, there are Valorence, Artisal, Wayah, and Mahani, and our kingdom Nitoriah. Of course Moon lives in a non-magical realm, it's where you're from, earth."

"Wait not Moon as in Moon Daniels . . . right?"

"Oh well I see you two have met, that'll save me introduction."

"She's so weird, she never talks to anyone. She's very artistic though. And she can sign very well too"

"Yes I image she is, your mother's family has always been talented. I know for a fact that you can write music very well, you play guitar like a professional and you can sing amazing as well"

"Thanks and I can sing okay but not amazing"

"So then now you see"

"See what?"

"Why she hasn't told or tried to prove that's she is a princess and that she has magical powers"

"Oh, yeah so she hasn't told anyone about whom she really is because she's afraid that they'll like her for who she can be instead of who she really is"

"So would you like to actually visit her? I have to show you how to summon a portal, so that you can go back and forth between worlds"

"Yea I'd like that, but can't you just use that door I came through to get here?"

"Well I guess so if you want to take the long way. Besides I thought you'd want to talk to your mom."

"Actually I do need to talk to her, so yea I'd like you to show me how to . . . summon a portal"

"Ok watch me, and then you try"

"Ok"

At first I couldn't tell whether he was concentrating or just goofy around then he looked down at the ground. He looked up, and said "Earth" then spread his hands apart. The next thing I know, there is a giant bluish purple circle and he stepped through it. It was awesome. I couldn't wait to try, but did he mean wait until he got back to try to or to just try whenever he was gone? I didn't care I just wanted to get back home to talk to my mom. So I done the exact thing I had just seen.

CHAPTER 24

Before I knew it I was in my bedroom looking at my mom. She was crying.

"Mom, are you ok?"

She looked up at me in a confused and relieved expression.

"Oh my God" you're ok. I was so worried about you I didn't know where you were . . . where were you!"

"Yes I'm ok; you're not the one that should be asking the questions"

"What are you talking about? I have the right to ask questions . . . you're my daughter for Christ's sake!"

"Oh so I'm your daughter now huh? I meet dad, he told me everything . . . I can't believe that you continue lie to me, like that mom!"

"Mackenzie Jo Delemorte, you will not talk to me like that you do understand?"

"What kind of question is that? Do I understand? Yes I understand . . . I understand a lot! Like the fact that you've been lying to me for the past 16 years of my life. I understand how you haven't even bothered to tell me who I really am! And I understand that you're not my real mom you're a liar!"

"I can't believe you . . . I can't believe you would talk to me like that, I am your mother, and I raised you for the past 16 years of your life!"

"But you still weren't going to tell me who I was huh?"

"I was I was just waiting for the right time . . . I couldn't tell you right away because I was afraid you'd want to leave to find your family, I couldn't lose you"

"But you lost me anyway . . . by not telling me the truth about who I was, if you would have told me earlier I would have understood, but you didn't instead I had to hear it from some weird old lady named Mrs. Crane"

"You've talked to Sicilia Crane?"

"If that's her first name then yes I have!"

"Oh my God . . . that means she's found you, we have to leave now! And I do mean now!"

"What why? What are you talking about now?"

"Just we have to go now!! Max I might have lied to you before but I'm telling you the truth now we have to go."

About that time we heard a giant explosion, I couldn't have been more than a mile down the road. Our house started to shake, we stumbled around but mom grabbed my arm and yelled basement. The next thing I know we were in the basement. Then she pulled me over into the corner and stuck her hand to the wall then there was a bright flash and we were in what I thought to be a cell. It was lined with red, purple, deep green, and pulses of bright blue. It was like I was inside a rainbow.

"What is this place?"

"Like I said we had to go . . . this might be the only place we're safe. But with one exception, how you have to use your power and put it in the cell. This is a protective cell but it's powered by magic. I'm afraid that my power alone won't be enough to protect us from Sicilia. She is more powerful than anything you could ever imagine. She's a sorceress and she draws her power off all the evil that takes place in your dimension, every evil deed multiplies her power by two."

"Yeah, then that's a lot huh?"

"Okay, I will . . . but how?"

"Just close your eyes. Focus on the pulse of magic, and then start weaving your magic into it. If you focus hard enough then it'll work"

"So pretty much I just have to imagine my magic pulsing through it and it'll work?"

"Yeah, pretty much . . . now hurry she's coming it won't be long before she gets here"

"Well I can't focus if you're yelling at me!"

"I'm not yelling! Okay fine, I'll just shut up"

"Okay, thank you"

CHAPTER 25

I couldn't believe what I was seeing, she was actually doing it; she was weaving her magic into the cell. Some mages that have trained for decades still can't do it perfectly. I always knew she was special but this, this is amazing! I couldn't believe it, there were pulsating colors of bright greens, blue's, yellow's, and orange's. There were also colors I've never seen before like; deep purple, maroon, bloody red, dark gray, deep orange and black. I'm for certain I've never seen black before. I doubt I've ever even heard of it before . . . wow.

"Am I doing it right? Max asked sounding very confused.

"Yes, you are, you are doing very well. I don't think I can even produce half as much power" I told her.

"Is that bad?"

"No, not at all, it's amazing. I don't think any of the guardians have that much power and they've been around for centuries"

"Okay"

"You need to hurry . . . she is coming, and she is extremely dangerous and-"

"And she is the one that killed my mom; the one that tried to kill me too, isn't she?"

"Yes, but how did you figure all that out?"

"I figured it out the first time she told me the story, if you would've seen all the rage and embarrassment in her eyes, you would've figured it out too"

"Oh, okay. Now hurry, I will help you but you need to try and go faster"

"Okay, I am . . . I am"

Just then I heard another explosion, and this time it sounded closer to the house, that is if we were even still in the house. I felt like I was getting stronger but it was probably just my imagination. The explosions were becoming closer together and louder.

"Oh my god she's coming . . . she's coming! Oh my god, can she get through?"

"Actually she's already here. The explosions are louder because she throwing her magic after the shield, the shield reflects attacks and it hits somewhere else."

"Awwwwwwwwwwwwwwww"

"Calm down Max or your magic will become unstable"

"Yeah, well that makes me feel so much better thanks" I screamed

"Hold on I'm going to transport us somewhere that when the shield breaks we'll have the advantage."

"What do you mean when it breaks; and what do you mean advantage?"

"The shield wonn't hold much longer even with both of our magic combined. Your just a beginner and don't know how to harness or enhance your magic. We'll need the advantage when it breaks because we'll have to fight to get away"

"Oh my God, what're we going to do?"

"We're going to stay calm and collective ok. Listen to me Max when then shield breaks you are going to run as fast as you can ok? And you're not going to stop no matter what happens alright."

"Ok but what about you?"

"Keep running, no matter what happens do you understand me?"

"Ok, fine I will keep running no matter what happens."

"I'm transporting us now."

The next thing I know we were in a field, in the distance I could see the castle. I wondered how long it would take to get there. Not long I hope. Then she appeared, the young woman Ms. Crane or Sicilia Crane. But she didn't look young and sweet like she had before, this time she had jet black hair with fiery red strikes. Dark red lips, red eyes. Her skin was pale white skin and looked like if it had never even see the sun. She wore a shredded black dress with red sleeves and black ankle boots. She looked terrifying. She was approaching us, as she raised her hand she started chanting something . . . it was the same chanting I'd heard in my dream. Then it hit me, she must have been the one in my dream, maybe it wasn't even a dream maybe it was a memory of some kind, I don't remember it happening to me; wait if what dad said was true then maybe since it happened to mom then it's her memory. That had to it.

"You are going to pay for burning me you little brat. No guardian will be able to protect you not even the little beginner like her" she said pointing to my mom.

"You're a guardian? Mom how could you not have told me this?"

"I'm sorry baby; I just didn't know how to . . . Awwwww!" she screamed as a bolt of lightning hits her in the back.

"Oh my God . . . mom please no! Please stop . . . don't hurt her, if you want me take me just stop!" I begged; I couldn't let her hurt my mom, even if she wasn't really my mom.

"Ok I will!" she said looking at me . . . she started to raise her hand, as lightning came shooting out I thought it was over just as it was about to hit me I felt a surge of power wash over me. I blacked out.

CHAPTER 26

I couldn't believe she dodged Sicilia's lightning, oh my God her eyes. Her eyes turned white as snow, she was levitating in the air above me. She started to raise her hands above her head and started chanting in Greek/Latin. I didn't even know she knew that language. She looked happy, like a little girl that just been given a lollipop for being good. It was freighting. All of a sudden she started screaming and each time she screamed and it got louder; Sicilia had what looked like bolts of lightning wrapping around her body, squeezing her tighter and tighter then, it stopped and everything became quiet, the only thing that broke the silence was the sound of Sicilia screaming in agony, begging Mackenzie to stop. This couldn't had been good, someone so sweet, so innocent, torturing someone, this way. When this was all over I was going to take her to the ancients to get their opinion on this. Just as Sicilia fell on the ground Max looked at me and started laughing, yea this can't be good. She fell out of the sky onto the ground, and started shaking like she was having a seizure of some kind. I got off of the ground and ran over to her body and knelt beside her. As I put my hand on her forehead and cast a spell to see if she was ok, her eyes fluttered open up.

"What happened?" she asked.

"You um, well you" I broke off mid sentence looking over at Sicilia's limp body that lay on the ground across from us.

"Oh my God will you please tell me I didn't do that! Please I didn't mean to I didn't know what I was doing I just . . . . i mean I just "I trailed off as I got up off of the ground and ran over to Sicilia's body and knelt down beside to check for any signs of life; a pulse, breathing . . . nothing. She was dead, and I killed. Oh my God how could I had done something like that.

CHAPTER 27

"How could I done something like that? I . . . I killed someone" I said as I started to cry.

"You didn't mean to, you couldn't control it." I wouldn't let her finished because I had already cut her off.

"That's the thing; I shouldn't been able to control it!" I screamed, she wasn't listening . . . I had just killed someone with magic and she was trying to say it wasn't my fault . . . even though it was my magic.

Magic or no magic Sicilia was dead . . . and it was because of me.

"Max stop blaming yourself, it wasn't your fault"

"Why wasn't it? Can you tell me that?"

"Because you're new to magic, you have yet to learn how to harness it. Your magic is stronger then you are. Do you think she cared how strong you or magic is? No, she didn't. The only thing she cared about is being dead."

"I guess you're right, but I still feel guilty"

"I know and that's normal; anyone with a heart would."

"I still feel awful though. Why couldn't I just let her live?"

"I know you do, and because if she would had live a lot more people would had died as well. Now let's get you to the ancients I think they might know why your powers took control of you."

"Where are they anyhow?"

"Follow me and I will show you"

"Ok"

We walked like seemed to be miles. By the time we had came upon a few giant rocks, we had stopped. I honestly didn't care what we were doing here, as long as I was able to sit down, because my legs were serious hurting.

I had to admit the scenery was beautiful. There were trees off to the left. You could see the castle if you turned your back to the rocks. I could even hear a river off in the distance.

"Ok we're here" she said

"We're where?" and what did Sicilia mean guardian?"

"I was hoping you had let that one slide. When you were an egg, I was assigned your guardian, by the superiors. You see a guardian is well a guardian; we use our magic to protect our chargers. 16 years ago when Sicilia announced her return, the superiors decided that, I would be your guardian. Since I knew that she would come for you I took you through a portal to earth and hid you there, where you would be safe"

"Oh ok . . . and superiors? I thought that we were going to see the ancients"

"We are, and the superiors are well superior to the ancients"

"So what is the difference?"

"The ancients are a group of people that has been around since the beginning of Nitoriah. The superiors are the ones that created Nitoriah and every other magical realm that exists."

"That is so cool"

"Yes it is . . . now remember don't speak unless your spoken to, stand up straight, and talk clear and polite and don't use your earth slang ok?"

"Ok . . . but why."

CHAPTER 28

J ust then one of the giant rocks moved, and out behind it came a group of people dressed in long dark blue velvet robes. There were 12 of them in total. The woman looked so graceful and beautiful. The men looked so, well, really cute, if they were the ancients they certainly didn't look the part. The one in the middle I decided was the leader. She had dark skin, long silky black hair pulled half way up; she had also had plump pink lips, beautiful caramel eyes, and looked like the youngest one there.

"Hello my name is Anthea . . . nice to see you Geneva . . . . i suppose you are Mackenzie . . . Ami am I right?" she said

"Yes, you are right" I replied

"Now why have you requested an audience with us Geneva?"

"Mackenzie's power; it over powered her . . . she has more powers then anyone of you and maybe even more then all of you all together. It was frightening. I would like to know what we're dealing with."

"What do you mean? What are we dealing with? She is not a creature she is a princess with an enormous amount of power" said Anthea sounding agitated

"I know . . . I did not mean any disgrace or offense"

"I know you didn't but I do see your concern, we shall test her at once to see what level of magic she possesses"

"Yes of course, Mackenzie you will do what lady Anthea asks alright?"

"Yes ma'am of course" I said in the most lady like voice I could muster."

"Alright then Mackenzie, follow me" said Anthea

"Yes ma'am and if you don't mind me asking how old are you exactly?"

"2,679 years old" she said sound amused

"But why do you look so young?"

"Because my mother the leader before me died 35 years ago I look young because in a way I am 23, you stop aging as fast as you become ancient. Since I became a ancient I now age 1 years per every 100 years."

"That's pretty cool" I said sounding seriously amazed.

"Yes, well I suppose it is . . . now what we are going to do is to take you back to our home and examine you and your magic . . . it will tell us how and why your magic over powered you, the source of your power, your power level and most importantly it will tell us what kind of magic you have and how to harness it" Anthea said

"What do you mean kind of magic?"

"I meant whether it's good or bad magic"

"But if I'm good doesn't that mean my magic is good?"

"Not necessarily . . . if your magic is bad it doesn't mean you are . . . you could be a saint yet your magic could be pure evil"

"So how do you control it then?"

"Well you have to use it in a good way" she said

"You can do that? I mean is that possible?"

"My dear anything is possible"

"Ok"

She took my arm and started to pull me to the black spot where the rock had been . . . then she stopped; froze dead in her tracks. In a way she looked like she was day dreaming except her expression changed and she looked like she was in pain.

"Are you ok?" I asked

"Huh? What? Yea I'm fine"

"What was all that for?"

"Oh you see ancients prophetic which means we can see into the future"

"So like a psychic?"

"No . . . psychics see small events in the near future, or they can get hints on something they want to know. Prophets can see anything that takes place at anytime; past, present and future."

"Awesome!"

"Yes"

"So what did you see?"

"That's not important right now . . . but if I'm right then we need to get them test done now . . . follow me"

"Alright"

CHAPTER 29

We walked through the blackness where the rocks were, and came into giant chambers. It had a huge stone table in the center; there were two doors off to the left and one massive door to the right. Each door was decorated, each has the crest I wore around my neck; a crescent moon with a single star hanging from it. They were beautiful.

"Mackenzie I need you to lay on that table over there ok?" Anthea asked pointing to the stone table

"Yes ma'am"

"I don't like it when you call me ma'am . . . it makes me feel old" she said laughing a little at her own joke

"Ok I'm sorry"

"Don't me . . . now when you lay down you need to stay very still . . . we're going to need to read some examines"

"What kind of examines?"

"Well first we're going to find out your power level"

"Alright" I said

I walked over to the table and laid down. Then she put one hand over my head and another over my heart . . . she started to mumble something in Greek as her hands illuminated.

"Ok I have a reading" Anthea said

"Ok . . . well what is it?"

"Your power level is . . . Wow 828 that's the highest I have ever read."

"So is that good?"

"Are you kidding me? Don't" That's amazing. I have to admit I'm a little jealous my power level is only 29"

"Oh I'm sorry"

"Don't be its ok"

"Is it true that the ancients made the magical realms?"

"Yes, it took 12 of us. Honestly it would only take 1 of you, to do what it took 12 of us to do"

"I'm sorry . . . so what's next?"

"It's ok and next we go through the door on the left"

"What are we going to do in there?"

"We're going to find out your power source and what kind of magic you have" she said

"Ok"

She lead me through the door on the left . . . inside was looked like a stadium. We walked down what seemed like 10 flights of stairs. At the bottom there were 3 ancients; two boys and one girl. The guy on the left had long sandy blonde hair pulled back into a loose pony tail at the end of the neck, bright green eyes, a beautiful set of lips, his face all together looked like it was sculpted by angels.

"What's his name?" I asked Anthea into a hushed tone

"My name is Avark, this is Atzel and Abira" he said in an angelic voice

Atzel was tall; had a tan, shaggy dark brown hair, big blue eyes and looked like a model. Abira now she was a totally different story she had curly fiery red hair, bright green eyes, freckles that covered her face, pale skin, pale pink lips, and wire rimmed glasses.

"Mackenzie Avark and Atzel will help us find out your power source, and Abira will find out what kind of magic you have" Anthea said

"I would like my power source determined first please" I said

"We can't do that" said Atzel also in an angelic voice

"Well why not?" I asked

"Because . . . we need to know what kind of magic you have, so we can knock out the power sources that don't correspond with your magic type" said Abira

"Fine but I won't like it" I said

"That's ok . . . we won't either" said Atzel

"No we won't said Avark

Abira led me to the middle of the stadium.

"What's your power level?" she asked

"102"

"Wow really? 102? I've never heard that one before but ok . . . Now I'm going to attack you, it is important that you react however you feel necessary . . . alright?"

"Yea but how will this help?"

"Whatever you use to defend yourself can be used to determine what kind of magic you have . . . I'm going to attack you multiple times alright"

"Ok"

She untied her cloak, and let it fall to the ground. She was wearing blue jeans and a t-shirt. She threw her hands out directly in front of her and started chanting in Greek\ Latin. It started raining, the raindrops turned to ice, and then turned razor sharp . . . I don't know how I did but I threw up a shield around me then started levitating. Abira looked frustrated at that but she joined me in the air. She shot razors out of her fingers; I threw up an extra shield and they all bounced back and hit the ground turning to cotton balls.

"So far it's good magic" Avark yelled up at us

"Ok" I yelled back; just then a giant rock slammed up against me then everything went black.

CHAPTER 30

I hoped I hadn't hurt her; she hit the ground so hard. And from that far up . . . Ouch if she's ok then she will definitely be sore tomorrow. I started to move toward her. A moment later she flew up; with her hands out in front of her, I felt pain; and lots of it. That's when I noticed her eyes; they were pitched black, like wholes in her head. I broke out of her hold as I started to levitate down, giant razor sharp rocks shot out of the ground; I had nowhere to go . . . I couldn't go down because of the rocks. I couldn't go up because of the stadium was made of rocks.

"Mackenzie, we have a verdict; you can stop now" I yelled

"Not yet" she said; her voice sounded like a thousand men were saying it with her. I had done it . . . I had released her power and it had again possessed her. I had to stop it before it got any worse.

"Mackenzie you're ok; you're safe . . . you can stop now"

"Not yet!" she yelled again with a terrifying voice . . . but this time it echoed.

What have I done? I have released a power that could kill us all . . . Oh my God! Lightning bolts were flying at me at full speed. Bam! They smacked into me just as I plummeted to the ground where there were razor sharp rocks. The last thing I remember is Mackenzie laughing.

I snapped out of it as Abira hits the rocks, and blood ran down them.

"NO!" I yelled. I wouldn't kill anyone else. I flew down to the ground I reach for her as Avark and Atzel looked at me.

"She's dead" Atzel said as Avark started crying

"My wife, you killed my wife . . . you need to be punished for what you've done" Avark yelled

I ran over to her body, she had a big hole in her chest. I fell across her chest as I started crying . . . all of a sudden I felt a wave of power wash over me. I sat on my knees; stuck my hands over my chest, when they started to glow I knew I could do it. I could heal her. The hole in her chest started to close. When it was completely closed; I concentrated harder if I could just get her heart and brain working she would be ok. I sat there for about 5 minutes concentrating when Atzel said "You can't do it . . . she's gone. Dead . . . you can't help her." Another burst of light shot out of my hands and into her chest then her eyes fluttered opened.

"I did it; I saved her!" I yelled as Avark pulled her into his arms and started to kiss her.

"I honestly didn't think you could do it, I owe you an apology . . . I'm sorry Mackenzie" Atzel said

"It's ok" I told him

"Thank you so much . . . I would have died without her" Avark said

"You're welcome . . . I'm for killing her in the first place . . . this is the second time my power has-"

"Possessed you" Abira said

"Exactly . . . I am sorry by the way"

"It's ok" she said.

"So do you want to go out sometime when this is all over?" Atzel asked

"How old are you?" I asked

"In ancients years in 18" Atzel said

"So he's younger than you? I asked Abira

"Who do you think broke him in?" she asked

"Yea I don't want to answer that . . . I'm just kidding" I said laughing

"So is that a yes?" he asked

"It's a definitely maybe" I told him

We both started smiling at each other . . . man he was cute. That's when I remembered.

"Oh my God . . . my date with Scott we were supposed to go out tonight . . . I need to get back . . . can we do this another time? Thanks" I didn't let them answer because I was already stepping through my portal.

Chapter 31

When I got home I looked over at my clock and read 6:50p.m. I only had ten minutes to get ready . . . no way was I going to have time to get ready.

I ran over to my closet and pulled out my favorite pale pink layered mini-skirt, and a cute black sequenced tank top. After I pulled them on I picked out a pair of ankle boots. Ran over to my dresser, opened my jewelry box and pulled out a white pearl layered necklace and pearl earrings to match. After I put them on, I knew I wouldn't have enough time to curl my hair, so instead I found a cute pick hair clip, and put it into my hair right above my ear. I looked at the clock on my way to the bathroom it was 6:57p.m. I had just enough time to brush my teeth. Just as I finished the door bell rang, I went down stairs, put on a smile and opened the door.

Scott looked handsome; he was wearing a red and black plaid shirt, blue jeans, white sneakers and a red cap. He was so cute; when he noticed what I was wearing he smiled and said" you look amazing"

"Thank you, Scott you're so sweet'

"You're welcome, why haven't you been at school lately? I thought that you was avoiding me . . . but I decided that I'd spend

2 hours picking out my best clothes even if you were going to stand me up" he said still smiling

I smiled back and then kissed him on the cheek and said, "I've been at my cousins house, her mom my aunt got into a car wreck . . . we were supposed to stay another week but I decided that you were to cute to stand up"

"Really?" he asked

"Absolutely"

"And I'm sorry for what I said"

"It's ok . . . so where are we going tonight?"

"Oh no I'm over dressed, do you think anyone will notice?"

"The only thing they'll noticed is how lucky I am to escort the prettiest girl in town to dinner" he said smiling

"Awe that's so sweet"

"It's only the truth"

"Have I mentioned how cute, sweet and charming you are? I asked him

"Not lately . . . no" he said as we both laughed

"So do you really think I'm pretty?"

"No . . . I think you're absolutely drop dead gorgeous, shall we go?" he asked

"Yes, we shall" I said

He took my hand and walked m out to his pick-up truck. It was nice. It was a red 4-door dodge pick-up truck. He had brought it two years ago when school had started. It cost him 15 years of saved money . . . like I said, it was nice.

"I love this truck" I said smiling

"Well if you're lucky you to ride in it a few more times . . . and if you're really lucky then you might even get to drive" he teased

"Oh really, ok; well I hope I'm lucky enough to get to go out with you a few more times"

"Trust me we'll both be lucky if that happens" he said as he shut the door, and walked around the truck and got into the drive seat and shut his door.

"To KC's chicken" he said as he started the truck.

We drove the rest of the way there with small talk and listening to country music. When we pulled in to KC's diner, Scott didn't put it into park he just sat there.

"Are we going to get out?" I asked

"In a minute, but first I have a question "he said

"Ok, ask away and I'll answer the question the best I can" I told him smiling

"Ok, we might not know each other really well but would you-" I cut him off I already knew where this was going.

"Go out with you? Will you let me answer after dinner? I'm starving and I have to know how you act on a date before I can answer"

"Ok, promise me you'll answer after dinner, when I take you home?"

"Yes, I promise" I told him

"Ok" he said

He got out and walked around the truck and opened my door for me.

"I might need help getting down, these heels aren't the best too walk in" I told him

"Ok, you do look beautiful though" he said as he put his hands on my waist and helped me down.

"Thanks you so much"

"You're welcome" he said

We held hands as we walked across the parking lot; then I realized that Tyler's vehicle was in the parking lot. But I didn't say anything.

CHAPTER 32

W hen we got inside, there weren't any open tables. We stood there for a while before two seats became opened at the bar.

"Follow me" I said pulling his arm

"Ok, I'm coming"

When we sat down, I picked up a menu

"The sea food, is the best thing here, as far as what I've tasted anyways"

"Ok"

The waitress came over and took our orders. I had ordered fish and chips, a chocolate milkshake, and a slice of apple pie; of course Scott ordered the same. We waited for about thirty minutes before our dinners were served.

"This looks amazing"

"It tastes even better" Scott said smiling

"I'll wait and see for myself" I said with a smile

"Ok, but prepare to get your socks knocked off"

"Oh trust me, I'm ready for anything"

"Ha-ha, okay then, we'll see"

"Yes, we will"

He was right, the sea food was amazing. The first bite was delectable, and it seemed to get better with every bite. The milkshake was so creamy; I couldn't help but think that the milkshakes could keep this place open for years. When we had both finished our food we started on the apple pie; and of course it was absolutely delicious!

"I want to come here, every date"

"Every date? So does that mean that we are going to go out again?"

"Ok, how's next week on Thursday?"

"Well actually, I have a family thing"

"So you ask me to take you out again then you reject me?"

I couldn't tell him about my family, it just, I can't. He would think I'm a freak, laugh at me and never speak to me again.

"I'm not rejecting you, I really do have a family thing, you see, I'm a, a uh"

"A princess and you have magic? I know already, and I don't care . . ." he said

"But how did you know?"

"Well you see I'm a prophet . . . actually I'm Abira's cousins, nieces, son, and I just happened to see you using magic in a battle against Abira'

"So you're magical too? Oh my God that's amazing!" I yelled, which got me a few dirty looks. When I realized how loud I had screamed it, I quickly laughed and said; man that book is going to be amazing! The few people that were staring looked away.

"Anyways, not really, my visions get in the way of things sometimes"

"So, it's still really cool"

"No actually, it's not"

"Why isn't it?"

"Because in the last vision I had, you were hollering for help and you were well laying over someone's body . . . you were unable to heal them"

"Whose body was it? I might be able to warn them"

"I can't tell you that . . . it would influence their fate, and you're not supposed to tamper with fate or destiny or anything like that."

"We're talking about life or death here Scott; now tell me who it was!"

"I can't" he said

"Why not"

"I've already told you why!"

"That's not good enough"

"If I tell you then I'll lose my magic. And you might lose your life for listening and influencing"

"So what's the big deal? I asked him

"The big deal is . . . I can't lose you! Nitoriah can't lose you! And like I said if you listen and try to influence it then it could be you who were dead, and me hollering for help! For Christ's sake Mackenzie would you just listen?" he yelled at me

"I am listening!" I yelled back

"Ok then just stop!"

"Ok but why?" I asked

"Because, Mackenzie you mean a lot to me . . . that's why I can't lose you . . . can you imagine how I would feel if you died?"

CHAPTER 33

I couldn't believe it . . . he cared about me! And this whole time he's been scared of losing me! Why couldn't I have just seen it? And he wants to know if I could imagine my own death? No, I can't, but I can imagine him dying because h tried to save me . . . I couldn't let that happen!

"Can you imagine how I would feel if you died?"

"No I can't . . . and how did you know it was me who died?" he asked sounding pretty confused

"Well you told me a few minutes ago; and again just now" I told him

"Oh ok, well I feel stupid now . . ." he laughed nervously

"It's ok, but since you already told me, that it was you who died can you tell me when and how?'

"I can't tell you when, since you already know it's me"

"Ok well . . . how? I insisted

"You were concentrating on something else, and I got a spell cast on me; but since I'm mortal and only have the power of prophecy, I don't know how to counter-act spells and it killed me"

"So why couldn't I heal you?"

"You can only heal if you really truly want to . . . and you didn't"
he told me as he started to cry.

"I'm sorry and it hasn't happened yet, please don't cry . . ." I
trailed off

"Why?" he asked

"Please, I don't want to die, I have a feeling that was supposed
to be together" I told him

"That's so-" he didn't finish . . . I thought he was having a
vision

"Oh my God!" he yelled, yup it was a vision.

"What? What happened?" I asked

"It wasn't me! It was Sicilia that died, and it was you who . . .
who cast the spell, you knew it was her disguised as me . . . even
when you snapped out of it you still knew it was her so you didn't
want to heal her" he said as fast as he could

"So then you don't die?" I asked

"No, I don't think I do" he said smiling

"Oh my God that's great, no wait a minute that's amazing!" I
told him

"Yes, so anyways, I should probably get you home"

"Ok, have you always had magic?"

"Yea I guess so . . ."

We drove home in silence; it was awkward now for some
reason. When we got back to my house, it was quiet.

"You can come in for a minute if you'd like"

"Sure, wait a minute where is your mom?"

"Nitoriah"

"Aw that explains why I don't smell brownies" he said
laughing

"I can make us some browning, ice cream sundaes, and even
cupcakes if you want" I said

"Ok . . . . are you sure you can make cupcakes and brownies?"

"Trust me you'll be bragging about 'em for weeks maybe even
months . . . they're delicious" I bragged but I couldn't help it.

"Oh really?" he asked

"Really"

"Well then why are you still standing here? You have brownies
and cupcakes to bake."

"You should pick out a movie for us to watch while the brownies are in the oven"

"Ok, do you have Saw; the final chapter? I've wanted to watch that movie lately"

"Yea and all the Halloween movies and my bloody valentine'

"Awesome" he yelled

"Yea I know right?" I said

"This is going to be great . . ." he said

CHAPTER 34

About 30 minutes later our ice cream sundaes were made, pop corn was popped, milk shakes were done. We were watching the movie and the brownies and cupcakes were in the oven.

"Wow you don't play around when it comes to ice cream; do you?"

"No, I sure don't"

"Good to know"

"Ok so what movie are we watching?" I asked him

"Saw: the final chapter . . . another question?"

"Awesome . . . that's a good movie; and what?"

"I've never been to Nitoriah do you think you could take me?"

"Yea sure; no problem do you want to go right now?"

"Sure let's go"

"Ok hold on a second. When the portal opens hurry up and step through it . . . then wait for me on the other side"

"Why can't you go to?"

"I am put a portal can only hold one person at a time"

"Oh well that sucks . . . will the portal let me through since I'm mortal?"

"You know what? I don't know; since you do have magical abilities you should be able to"

"Ok; well I guess there really is a first time for everything huh?" he said nervously

"Yea I guess so" I told him offering a smile

"Ok let's do this"

"Wait I have to check on the brownies and cupcakes"

"Oh yea . . . hurry"

"Ok"

I ran into the kitchen and pulled open the oven . . . yes! They are down, so I pulled them out of the oven. Then I pulled out some vanilla icing and iced the cupcakes. Then I pulled out some fudge icing and covered the brownies with it. When they were finished I cut them, placed them on a plate, and placed them on the kitchen table.

"Ok, they are done, I didn't let them cool, so they are probably not the best" I said walking back into the living room . . . I froze dead in my tracks.

"Scott! No! let him go please he hasn't done anything wrong" I yelled.

CHAPTER 35

The next thing I saw was someone in a black cloak slashed Scott's throat, then Scott's limbed body crumbled to the floor.

"No!" I screamed as tears ran down my face.

"He didn't do anything wrong!" I yelled as I levitated off the ground. I rose my hands out in front of me at waist level and started screaming . . . each time it got louder and each time black cloak got closer to the ground. When they were on their hands and knees I stopped screaming, I stepped out of the air and onto the blood soak carpet. I walked over to black cloak and pulled their hoods off their head.

"Atzel . . . how could you? Oh my God, you're supposed to be the good guy!"

"Mackenzie I couldn't help it . . ."

"I don't care what you say, you hurt him! You have to decide, back up and let me hear him, or you can prepare yourself for battle"

"I can't let you heal him"

"Then you best prepare yourself for battle!" I screamed as I ran over to Scott's body and knelt beside him . . . he still had a pulse but it was growing weak, fast." Hang in there" I said.

"What are you doing?" Atzel screamed as I got up off the floor and walked toward him.

"You will see" I said as he hit the wall on the other side of the room.

"Stop . . . Don't! I'm sorry!" he pleaded

"It's a little too late for that Atzel, don't you think?"

I couldn't wait to do this I thought, as he started flying across the room hitting every wall in the living room. After about 4 minutes of being tossed around like a rag doll, he started to bleed so I stopped and walked over to him on the other side of the room. I bent down and saw that it was his nose that was bleeding . . . bummer. I picked up the knife that was on the floor beside him and sliced it across his forehead.

"Now we are talking" I said laughing a little. I ran my fingers across the cut, pulled them up to my mouth and before I could think about it again I licked the blood from my fingers.

CHAPTER 36

A lot of memories flooded into my head; but they weren't my own . . . they belonged to Atzel. There were memories of him killing innocent women and children. He spent hours in his champers; at the ancient's home planning ways to kill Scott. The world would be done a favor, if I killed him right now, but it wasn't his destiny. His destiny wasn't to die by my hand and I knew that. I would let him bleed until he was near death, and then I would heal him. I got up off the ground beside Atzel, and walked over to Scott's lifeless body, knelt beside him stuck my hands over his chest, and my hands started glowing . . . he was healing, I could feel his pulse getting stronger. Then he reached up and grabbed my hand "why did you save me? He asked.

"Because I don't want to lose you either" I told him smiling.

I helped him up off the floor then I walked over to Atzel whose body lay on the ground, sat down beside him too. "Thank you my love" he said smiling. That smile didn't stay very long because I slapped it off of him. "You jerk . . . don't EVER call me LOVE AGAIN! Do you understand me?" I asked

"Yes, I guess so . . . but answer me this . . . how can you choose some filthy mortal over a pure-breed ancient?" Atzel asked.

"Hey pal I don't know what your problem is but you will not talk to her like that, and I am tired of you treating me that way"

"Atzel I chose him because he's not a jerk like you!" I said looking over at Scott. "And Scott this does not concern you!" I barked

"Sorry Max" Scott said

"It's ok" I smiled

"Oh brother, why do I have to keep getting rejected?" Atzel asked.

"Well maybe it has to do with all those innocent women and children you killed, or maybe it's the fact that you go around planning to kill your own brother, did you ever think about that?" I asked

"You know I did, but then I figured I could just do this" he said as lightning shot toward me.

I stepped back once then I threw up a shield, the lightning bounced back and shot into Atzel chest, he stumbled backwards exploding into a show of lights and colors then fell into a pile of dust.

"So much for being cremated, I joked

"That's not funny" Scott said

"I know I just thought-" he cut me off

"That you'd lighten the mood about a guy getting cremated by his own lightning bolt . . . yeah your hilarious" he said sarcastically

"Sorry I didn't mean to make matters worse . . . I'm sorry"

"For what . . . killing a guy or flirting with him? Yea I seen that in a vision too"

"Well first of all it was either him or me, and I decided that I wasn't going to die today; especially if there was a change that he would torture you when I was gone . . . and second of all I never flirted with him!" I yelled

"So what was it then? He just decided that he would practically kill me for no reason at all?"

"I don't know! I don't know what was going on in his twisted head alright?" I said

"Alright well I'm going home now, before you turn me into dust too" he said angrily

"I can't believe you just said that to me!" Get out of my house" I yelled at him in disbelief.

"Fine, I don't want to be here with you anyways!" he said leaving the living room heading for the door.

"Great, the guy I thought was the nice one, turned out to be as bad as the bad guy" I said as he walked through the door.

When he was gone I walked back in the living room, and looked at the blood soak carpet. Mom wasn't going to be happy; her brand new white carpet turned blood red . . . literally. She was going to kill me. I guess I had better get to work. But first, I have to go change.

About five minutes later, I had my hair in a pony tail, rain boots on, as well as blue jeans shorts and a plain blue t-shirt.

"Ok here goes nothing" I said to myself.

I walked into the bathroom; got the foam carpet clean, window wash, pine sol, the mop, 4 sponges and a bucket of steaming hot soapy water.

After I had gathered all of my supplies, I took it into the living room. Got down on my hands and knees and started scrubbing the floor. After about an hour of scrubbing, I finally decided that I would clean up Atzel's ashes, so I went back into the kitchen, got a broom and swept up his ashes. I then proceeded to throw them away.

After about 3 hours of non-stop cleaning the living room was back to the way it was, so I went back upstairs to the bathroom to take a shower.

5 minutes after I got in the shower there was a knock on the door.

"Crap!" I said as I turned off the water and got out of the shower.

When I got back to my room I threw on some red pajama shorts, and a baby blue tank top, then checked my clock, 11:30 p.m.

Knock! Knock; who would be at my door at 11:30 at night? Who would be stupid enough to be here this, late?

CHAPTER 37

I hope she answers the door" I whispered to myself.

Dear God, I mean I knew she was mad but seriously? Oh, well since she probably isn't answering for anyone I mine as well leave.

I turned away from the door and started walking to my truck, and then I heard someone running inside the house.

"Mackenzie, are you ok? What happened? I asked frantically

"What? What are you talking about? The door bell was . . . wait let me guess, that was you wasn't it?" she asked sounding confused

"Yeah . . . I turned around when I went past KC's diner. I shouldn't have treated you like that"

"Yeah by the way why did you treat me like that?" she asked confused

'Because you killed my brother, how else am I supposed to act? I am sorry for treating you that way Mackenzie, I was a jerk"

"Yes you were" she screamed

"I know this! Just because your life is prefect doesn't mean you have to rub it into everyone else's face!" I yelled back at her not realizing what I had said until after I said it!

"Wait what? She demanded

"I said you don't have to rub your prefect life into everyone else's faces"

"Why would you do that to me? My life is not prefect and I don't rub it in anyone else faces"

"Yes you do! And yes it is! Especially me, you treat me like crap, you might not realize it but you do"

"Oh my God, I am so sorry I had no idea you felt that way-" I cut her off

"Please . . . don't be, I am just up set and that gives me no reason to be a jerk, I am so sorry Mackenzie"

"Oh no, I am sorry to"

"Don't be"

"But I am, do you still want to take a trip to Nitoriah?"

"I want to, I really do but I can't . . . I have too many things I got to do, I can't tell you what they are, and I would feel like I was betraying you"

"You can tell me anything"

"I know but I can't"

"Well why not?" she asked in the saddest puppy dog eyes I've ever seen in my life.

I can't lie to her but I can't tell her either. "I think we should just spend time together, because when all my secrets unravel you are going to hate me"

"Please . . . I'm sorry; I can't do this on my own, run my country and control my powers to."

"You won't be on your own; you'll have your tutors, Natalya, your dad and your ancients"

"But I don't have you . . . I know I have all of those people, but you're my friend, you know me better than any of them . . . please?"

"I really shouldn't but I guess I can go with you for a little while"

He's acting a little strange; I wonder what he's not telling me . . . wait a minute, I could see the entire past on Scott's brother Atzel, just by tasting his blood. I wonder why that was. If I can cut Scott, then I'll be able to see what's he's hiding right?

"Hey Scott, while you're here, I need help cutting the cake, would you mind?"

"No, that sounds easy enough . . . so can I have a piece while I'm in here?"

"Yea . . . and could you bring me a piece to?

"Yea sure . . . what's wrong?"

"My head is just swimming but I'll be fine, I'm going to go in the living room and lay down on the couch ok?"

"Yea sure thing, do you want me to get you an aspirin?" he asked

"Yes that would be great . . . Scott, thank you so much" I said trying to sound as if I were in a little pain.

"You're very welcome"

"You're amazing . . . do you know that?"

"I do now, so go in there and lie down" he said pointing to the living room.

"Alright . . . and thanks again"

"No problem"

I walked toward the living room, pausing long enough to look back at Scott and offer him a slight smile. He really was sweet I couldn't believe I was lying to him, but drastic times cause for drastic measures.

When I got into the living room I went over to the couch and lay down. I was so tired, and the couch was so soft . . . before I knew it I was drifting off into a deep sleep.

CHAPTER 38

I was walking through the snow, trying to find something. As I turned to my left I seen something blue coming out of the snow, I found it, I had found her; I ran over to the blue, and pulled her out of the snow. She was so pale, so cold; I had to heat her up. I pulled off my glove stuck it to her chest and started chanting "Ut spiritus vobis calor accipere calor ampleti" my hands started to glow, her color was returning and her breathing was becoming steadier. She was warming up; what a relief. I heard yelling for help, I looked around me and didn't see anyone. Then I heard it again, and again. "Is anyone out there? If you need help tell me where you are . . . please I can help you" I yelled. "Help m please, I don't know where I am, I'm so cold, I'm in so much pain, I can't move; please help me" a small voice said. "Hold on I'm coming just keep talking to me and I'll be able to find you. I yelled in response. I looked down at the little girl that lay curled up in my lab "I'll be right back Max I promise" I said to her, just as I looked up, I was jerked awake.

"Mackenzie . . . . wake up" Scott was saying.

"I'm awake, what's wrong?"

"Nothing, you were sweating and screaming so I assumed you were having a nightmare, so I woke you up" he said

"Oh ok, thanks" I told him

"No problem, so what was it about?"

"What was what about?" I asked suddenly confused

"Your dream, what was your dream about?" he said laughing

"Oh, right yea . . . well I was a woman walking through a bunch of snow, found a girl, pulled her out of the snow, warmed her back up then I called her . . . I called her Max and then I just left her there to find someone else who was hollering for help'

"Oh, and her name was Max?"

"I don't know, but that's what I called her"

"That's bizarre huh?" he asked

"Yea . . . I would say a little bit, but this is a big bit"

"Ok so are we going to find out who you were in the dream or not?"

"What, how can we do that?"

"It's called dream traveling, kind of like space travel but only you don't have a time limit"

"Oh, that is awesome! So how do we do it?"

"That's the tricky part; we have to go to Nitoriah, travel to the valley of no return, and find a stone"

"What's a sage stone? And where at in, *the valley of No Return* is it?" I asked him

"It is a stone that enables dreams travel and it is found in the cave of lost souls guarded by lightening wraiths"

"Wraiths as in like spirits that can possess stuff?"

"Yea it's something like that"

"So you mean you want to kill something that's already dead?"

"Yeah pretty much"

"And you think I should put my life on the line for a dream?"

"That's your choice not mine, but answer me this, do you remember any of your childhood?"

"Bits and pieces, but for the most part they're only of Christmas, thanksgivings, and birthdays"

"Ok so what if, one of your dreams can help you find out or remember more of your childhood?"

I stood there a moment and just thought about it, he was right. Besides, I have always wanted to remember my childhood.

"Ok how do you kill them?" I asked

"You'll need holy-water"

"Of course I should've guessed" I said sarcastically

"Wraiths are evil spirits; they can only be killed by pure good"

"So why can't I just use my magic?"

"We could but you were never told if it was good magic or not"

"Oh yea so I can't use my powers?"

"No, unfortunately not"

"Why?"

"Because if your magic is bad it will strengthen the wraith and its powers"

"That sucks huh?"

"Yea, we have to go and find out your test results"

"Can we bring holy-water too?"

"Yea sure"

"Ok but can we go to Nitoriah tonight and go to the caves tomorrow?"

"Yea your rights, besides churches are not open this late"

"Wait I might know one that is"

"Which one"

"The one I go to"

"Which one is that?"

"Saint John's catholic church it's in town by Jane's supermarket"

"Ok, but I didn't know you went to church"

"Yea there is a lot you don't know yet, I think we should just be friends for now"

"I told you so"

"Wait, earlier you said I was going to kill Sicilia for good remember?"

"Yea, I do, and yea I did"

"I've already killed her"

"Oh right; Geneva hasn't told you about that yet have she?"

"Tell me what?"

"Right, well in order to kill evil you have to kill it by all the elements"

"Could I just kill the wraiths like that?"

Ok listen very closely, you can only kill evil being completely by all the elements, but in order to kill evil creatures you need pure good"

"Oh ok, now I get it . . . . I think. Wait how do you know all this?"

"Abira tutored me in the magic ways long ago, because all the prophets need to know in case their guidance or assistance is needed"

"Cool so can you teach me?"

"No"

"Well why not?"

"Because royals have teachers and tutors for that"

"Why did you say it like that?"

"Because, you've always had it easy and probably always will"

"So, that's just an opinion, and that doesn't mean it's true"

"Ok sure, why do you think Natalya is so stuck up?" he asked sarcastically

"Because . . . . she was raised a royal . . . but I wasn't and you know that"

"So that doesn't mean all that power and wealth won't go to your head"

"It WON" T and I can't believe you would say that"

"It always happens"

"No it doesn't, ok maybe it does but that won't happen to me, do you know why?"

"Why"

"Because I can run my country from here in Ackerman"

"No you can't"

"Well why not?"

"Because during your coronation you have to decide whether you want to stay in Nitoriah, and be a princess and never come back to earth or you can stay on earth and lose all of your powers and your princess title and be by yourself"

"I won't be alone, I have Geneva"

"That's another thing, she's a guardian of the moon or the royal family, if you lose your title you are no longer a royal and she has to leave to get assigned to her next charge"

"But that's not fair"

"If you think about it, it kind of is"

"How"

"I don't know, now are we going to church or not?" he asked
stubbornly

"Yes, I guess we are"

"Ok then, let's go"

CHAPTER 39

We walked out to his truck without a word. He again opened the door for me and helped me in, I told him thank you but he just said "No problem." He didn't say anything else all the way there, and I wasn't about to say anything. About 5 minutes after leaving my house we were pulling into the churches parking lot.

"We're here" I informed him

"Yea, I kind of figured that one out on my own"

"Really . . ." I said being sarcastic

"Yea well, it was the giant stain glass window that shows images of famous bible scenes that gave it away"

"Oh, so you mean you figured all that out on your own without even looking at the wooden sign beside the door that says "St. John's Catholic Church"

"Oh, I didn't even see the sign, even though its almost the size of the door!" he yelled sarcastically

"Oh, so how'd you miss that? I always knew you needed contacts; but that's only because you wouldn't look good in glasses" I said trying to be smart

"You don't have to get smart alright"

Yes . . . it worked. I guess I'm just that good, ha now only if I could cut him.

"You're right, I'm sorry . . . could you ever forgive me?"

"Yes I could, and I already have" he said, putting a little extra attitude on the word could.

"That's good so are we going inside?"

"Are you wearing that inside?"

"Well yea, because I think he might suspect someone who has never been to his church asking for a lot of holy water don't you think? So how much do we need?"

"A few gallons"

"Gallons . . . this just keeps getting better and better doesn't it?"

If I'm with you, then yes it does" he said smiling

"Awe that's so sweet, don't press your luck boy, I'm still mad at you for saying that to me"

"Hold a grudge much?" he asked sarcastically which just made me madder

"Shut up . . . you jerk!? I yelled as I heard a door open. We both gasped in shock.

We both turned to see an old man about in his sixties who had white thinning hair, brown eyes, alabaster skin, and a long white robe.

"Reverend Simmons" I yelled running toward him as he turned around.

"Mackenzie, what a lovely surprise I was just looking up . . . so what can I do for you?"

"I need holy water"

"Oh, alright, well how much do you need?"

"A few . . ."

"A few, what my dear?"

"A few, uh gallons" I said

"Oh, oh . . . ok um yes I think I have a few gallons in the back, follow me"

"Ok and thank you"

"You're very welcome" He said smiling

I turned to Scott which was still standing there. "Come on Scott, let's go you dork" I yelled

"I'm coming give m a minute ok?"

"Ok I will" he said as I turned around and followed reverend Simmons into the church.

I hope this isn't the reverend Simmons I've heard of . . . as I was walking toward the church I heard Mackenzie screaming.

"Hold on Mackenzie" I yelled running into the church, but how do you find someone in a church you're never been to?

"Wait a minute my visions . . . maybe if I can summon up the power then I can force a vision to find her" I thought to myself, but how do you summon the power? Wait Abira told m, if only I can—get it I know how.

I sat cress-cross on the floor put my pointer fingers to my temples, and focused on my power source 'love' if only Mackenzie knew.

I heard her scream again so I focused harder, all of the sodden I jumped up and started running within seconds I was want Mackenzie.

CHAPTER 40

"Scott, I'm so glad you're here, reverend Simmons is a . . . is a-" He cut me off, but I was thankful, besides I didn't really know what he was.

"Xivilia, a powerful and rich servant of Hades or Satan"

"Wait what? So can you kill it?"

"No, but look out" he yelled, as I felt something stab me in the back of my neck.

"Scott, tell Natalya I give her the throne to her" I said nervously

"You can heal yourself, guess focus on your power source"

"But I don't know what my power source is"

"Its love like my, why do you think your eyes turn white when you killed Sicilia the first time?"

"I guess, but how do I focus on my power source though?"

"Just focus on someone you love"

"Ok"

She laid there with her eyes closed when her pulse was weakening I jumped for Scott, to birds with one stone. Master was going to be pleased when he hears I killed the white dragon and her power source.

Before I could get my hands on him, Mackenzie jumped up off the floor and pulled a thing of holy water off of her pocket and sprayed me with it.

"No! please, stop the burn!" I pleaded

"No! You can tell your master that I can't wait to meet him because his going to died too"

"Please don't I tell you?"

He couldn't finish his sentence because he had already exploded into red dust and then disappeared. I turned to Scott as he hugged me and whispered in my ear "I knew you could do it"

"Because of you; so how exactly did you know my power source?"

"Well . . . my power source has always been love I just needed to find it"

"Wait you lied to me!" I yelled

"No I just didn't tell you"

"Ok whatever . . . so that doesn't explain how you knew my power source"

"Exactly it does, love is the trickiest power sources out there . . . before that first date I never had visions ; that was because in order for my kind of power source to work you need a second person with the same source, and they also have to truly love you and you have to truly love them"

"Wait you're saying you did this to me, made me this way?"

"No I did not; you've always been like this I just kind of had to activate it"

"So you did this to me?" I demanded

"Yes and no"

"Ok whatever so do I have to kill this guy again?" I said pointing to spot where reverend Simmons had been a moment ago.

"None you sure don't"

"Alright good" I said happily

"Ok let's get out of here" he said grabbing my hand. Then I started feeling pain, and a lot of it at that, and then I blacked out.

CHAPTER 41

She fell to the ground and started shaking like she was having a serious seizure. I knelt down beside her on the ground and asked; "Mackenzie are you ok?"

I turned her face toward me and saw that she had blood coming from her eyes, and then I heard slashing noises as she started to bleed all over.

"Mackenzie, please don't! I love you, you can't do this to me!" I yelled at her holding her head in my hands.

"Scott, help me" I heard someone whisper but Mackenzie's mouth wasn't moving.

"Please leave her alone! She hasn't done anything wrong"

"Help me and I'll save her Scott"

"No Sicilia I will not help you, you Shea devil!"

"Then she will die" she said calmly

"You evil witch you better help her or I'll kill you for good . . . personally!"

"You will not talk to your mother that way . . . do you understand me?"

"You listen to me you Shea demon, you may have given birth to me; but you are not! And I mean not! My mom"

110

"If you anger me anymore she will die faster than you ever thought possible, do you understand me?"

"Yes! If I bring you back do you promise you will save her?"

"I can't do that"

"Promise me mother! You don't want someone else to heal her then have the chance to kill her do you?"

"What are you talking about?"

"Am sure Atzel will love to get some revenge for Mackenzie for killing his mom and then killing him"

"No she killed me" bring me back! So I can heal her and bring my son back! That way when she's back in full health we can torture her together"

"Promise me you will wait until she is well again before you do anything alright?"

"Ok, ok whatever"

"Promise me"

"Ok I promise"

"Ok, hold on a second"

I stuck my palm of my left on my forehand and healed my right hand out in the air as if holding someone's hand after I said her name the tenth time.

"Thank you my child"

"She said laughing"

"Now heal hr please . . . she is my entire heart, I know you have always been disappointed in me but please mom I love her"

"Alright, and I've never been disappointed in you; you're just like your father in every way, and I've always felt like I felled him because I was unable to heal him like I was you"

"Really"

"Really, move aside, I'll heal her if she really means that much to you, but you do realize who exactly she is right?"

"Yea, Mackenzie, princess and true heir to the throne of Nitoriah"

"She's the white dragon"

"What? You're lying to me, how could you? Just heal her and leave please!"

"You'll learn I am right in time my son" she said as she stuck a hand on top of mine, which was still on Mackenzie's forehead, and the other one on top her heart, then started to heal her. A few minutes later her eyes fluttered open and my mother had vanished. I didn't care where she had gone, because Mackenzie was okay.

"Scott . . . I'm glad I got you in my life" she said as tears ran down her cheeks, while I was sitting her up.

I kissed her cheek and whispered "I'm glad to have you in my life as well" into her ear.

Chapter 42

I turned around and put my head on his chest, and started to cry. Then it hit me . . . "Um Scott, how could you heal me? You don't have that kind of power, do you?"

"No I don't have any powers and it was Sicilia who . . . who healed you" he said pushing me away

"How could you let her anywhere near me!" I yelled

"I didn't have a choice; I don't want to lose you"

"How does she know who you are? No wait how did she come back?" I asked but he wouldn't look at me and started to get up . . . now's my chance. I pulled the knife out of my pocket and sliced open his palm . . . then I stuck it to my mouth and started to drink, as his memories flooded into my head. Then I stopped.

"She's your mother, and you brought her back using my own powers . . . how could you do this to me, betray me like that?" I demanded

"I told you I had no choice, I wasn't going to lose you!"

"You lied to me, and look at me!" I yelled

"No . . . I can't"

"You will" I said as his head turned toward me

"What are you doing to me?"

"What are you talking about?" I asked as I seen he was crying, and struggling to turn away but couldn't

"I don't have control over my body! That's what I'm talking about . . . now could you please let me go?" he asked worriedly

"Yea sure, you can have control over your body back" as I said he turned away again, I heard a faint whisper from Scott saying

"Thanks"

Scott started to walk away when he hit the ground holding his head screaming. I got up off the ground and ran over to him; I put one arm around his back and the other on top of his head, calmly and gently saying "It's alright"

I don't know how it happened but he was on his side in a fetal position, slightly crying.

"Scott, are you ok?" I asked

"Huh/ Oh um yea, I think so" he said still whimpering

"I looked . . . in your head, you were having flash backs of when you were a child weren't you?"

"Yea, my dad was being killed in front of me and all I could do was cry"

"I know and before you even say it, you're not the same helpless child anymore, you can do something about it all now, wait didn't you say you have to kill someone with all the elements before they're truly dead?" I asked curiously

"Yes but that's magical beings, well immortal ones anyways, he was mortal, that's how I'm mortal but have magical abilities"

"Could there be a way for you to become immortal?"

"I don't think so, but if there is either Serena or Sage would know"

"Who are Serena and Sage?"

"Superior's their names all start with an S believe it or not, just like all the Ancients names start with an A"

"That's unique, I guess"

"It actually is"

"So how do we find them?"

"We don't, you go to the fountain of eternal life and ask Aisha the youthful fairy for an audience with them, and if you're important enough then they'll see you"

"Wow so a harmless fairy, guards the fountain?"

"Trust me, from what I hear she's *far* from harmless"

"I guess I will just have to see for myself huh?"

"I guess so, wait you don't even know how to get there"

"That's why you're going with me . . . . to Nitoriah"

"Really?" he asked.

"Yes, really; now let's go"

"Wait shouldn't we summon a portal behind the building? Humans aren't supposed to know about magic"

"No worries, if anyone sees anything, everyone will think they're crazy"

"I guess you're right"

"Yeah, but just in case let's summon one behind your truck . . . okay?"

"Okay"

We walked over to the side of his truck that was facing the church, and made sure no one was around then I called forth a portal and he stepped through, and it closed. I looked around to make sure the coast was clear then summoned one for me and stepped through.

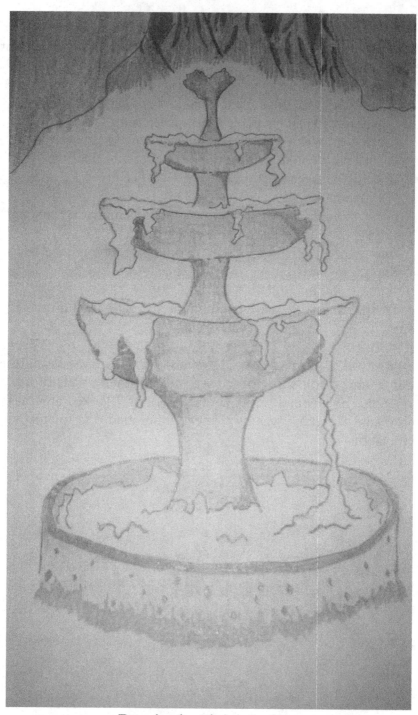

Drawing by Christy Jenkins

CHAPTER 43

⊕ nce on the other side I saw Scott looking around in awe.

"You okay there Scott?" I asked him

"I'm just fine, so this is Nitoriah huh?" I didn't answer because I knew that was a rhetorical question.

"Okay, so how do we get there?"

"Follow me" he said as he started off toward the woods. After a few miles we came upon a rock which held a giant wooden gate.

"So how do we get in?" I asked

"We find the answers to the riddles"

"Which riddles?"

"Those" he said as a giant breath-taking purple, blue, and green feathered bird flew over head dropping a piece of paper.

"What kind of bird was that?" I asked now in awe

"A phoenix, rare and very beautiful birds"

"Okay, so what do the riddles say? And how many are there?"

"They ask about living and eternal life, and there are four of them"

"Okay so what are they?"

"The first riddle is; three lives I have, gentle enough to soothe the skin, light enough to caress the sky, hard enough to crack rocks, of what form am I?"

"Okay so maybe if we just skip the first part we can make a category of all the living things for each part and the one that's in all three is the answer"

"Sounds good to me, do you have a pen and paper?"

"No, but I can make some" I told him smiling slyly.

"Okay"

"Pen, paper" I said loudly a clearly a moment later I had both.

"Okay, now what are things that are *gently enough to soothe skin?*" he asked, more to himself than to me.

"Mud or earth, you know like mud baths"

"Okay, so mud, what else?"

"Well let's see, what about air and water?"

"I understand water but air?" he asked looking confused.

"You can't feel it, so you can't complain that it hurts right?"

"I guess so, so we got earth, water and air. So is that all?" he asked

"Yeah, that's all I can think of" I told him.

"Okay, next part, *light enough to caress the sky*"

"Okay so air is kind of the sky, so I'm going to say dirt and water, dirt or sand can be put into the sky . . . sand storms. Water can be steam and even water vapor" I said smiling.

"True so next, hard enough to crack rocks; earth can't crack itself . . . can it?"

"No I don't think it can, but what about water? I mean there's water erosion, right?"

"Yeah, so then there is your answer, water also has three lives if you think about it, regular, frozen and steamed" he said

"You're right, so the first answer is water"

"Okay, next riddle; I am, in truth a yellow fork, from tables in the sky, by inadvertent fingers dropped, the awful cutlery. And mansions never quite disclosed, and never quite concealed, the apparatus of the dark, to ignorance revealed . . . that's the hardest one for now" he said looking thoughtful.

"Maybe not, I think its lightning. I mean think about it"

"I think you might be onto something"

"Really" I asked sarcastically

"Really, it's *like a yellow for. Tables from the sky* could be clouds. I don't know about the *by inadvertent fingers dropped. The awful cutlery,* it certainly could be an awful way to die. The *mansions, concealed and disclosed,* I don't know about that part either. *The apparatus of the dark* could be the light in the dark. *To ignorance revealed,* that could be like when you go out into a lightning storm with an umbrella; you're just asking to get electrocuted" he said proud of himself.

"That's true, so the second answer is lightning"

"Okay, the third one says; I am one to be watched; I'm known as a great forder of water, I'm the perfect example of understanding"

"Okay, *I am one to be watched, a crystal.* They're breathtaking, so you like to look at them or a crystal ball"

"Alright, then *I'm known as a great forder of water,* a result of a water transformation"

"*I am the perfect example of understanding,* the understanding of how something so beautiful can be so simple"

"Yeah that's true too, okay so the answers we know of so far are water, lightning and crystal. What's next?"

"Okay the final one says: *to wonder around, mainly comes in the form of bills, used as an extra arm or foot for a monkey, the fifth month of the year, known as characteristics, my whole is eternal life*" he said sounding very puzzled.

"Well um, to wonder around is to roam" I said

"And mainly mail comes in the form of bills" he replied

"Um, a tail is used as an extra arm or foot for monkeys"

"The fifth month of the year is May" he said then added "A trait could also be a characteristic"

"My whole is eternal life, wait didn't you say one of these is about immortality? What if that is the answer to this one?" I asked

"We would be taking a risk on this but there is a really good chance that you're right, we'll just have to find out then wont we?" he said knocking on the door. It opened and a little girl appeared. She was cute, had long curly brown hair pulled back into ponytails on the sides of her head, she had freckles, caramel brown eyes, alabaster skin and salmon skin. "Do you have the answers?" she asked in the sweetest voice I have ever heard.

"Yes, I think we do" I told her

"Okay, well what are they?"

"They are water, lightning, crystals, and immortality"

"Well I'm sorry . . . . that you had to wait so long, those answers are correct"

"Thank you, so can we go through?"

"Yes, be my quest, walk through the door and stay on the path, alright?"

"Yes, thank you again" I told her

"You're welcome"

CHAPTER 44

We walked past her but when I turned around to ask her name and her age, she was gone. I turned and looked at Scott, who had laughed a little and said "She is a warrior fairy in training, her name is Shaleigh and she is 11"

"Oh and how did you know I wanted to ask her all of that?"

"The look on your face when you turned around gave it all away" he said smiling

"Oh, well duh"

We walked for about five minutes down the path before coming up to a fountain which had been frozen, so it didn't run, when I bent over to sit down on the ground beside it; a little blue orb of light, floated down from a heart shaped stone on top of the fountain.

"My name is Destiny but I am also known as Fate, and I am the youthful fairy as well as the guardian of eternal life" a small voice said as the light went away and a small person grew to my size.

She was one beautiful fairy; she had honey colored skin, big bright blue eyes like eyes, dark pink lips, and long dark brown hair, with strips of blue that matched her eyes. She was wearing a white tube-top and a short flowing skirt, which was connected by blue lace ribbons. Her gorgeous hair was pulled up half way, the bottom half was completely banana-curled. The half that was pulled up was twisted into a small bun.

"It is nice to meet you Destiny" I said smiling

"And you as well" she said in return

"I suppose you know why we are here?" I asked

"Yes, I do, why else would you come to the fountain of eternal life?"

"Fair enough"

"Who may I asks wants an audience with the superiors?" she asked but before I could answer Scott had pulled her aside and was explaining something to her. A few minutes later she looked at me with frightened eyes, I smiled which just seemed to make her more nervous.

When they returned she frantically asked "The superiors would be more than happy to see you they would be happy, they would be honored"

"Honored?" I asked suddenly confused.

"I'm sorry; did I use the wrong word? I can think of a different one if you wish"

"What is going on here?" I demanded

"Your majesty, the superiors will explain everything" Aisha said without looking m in the eyes.

"Well will you take us too them, please?" I asked

"Oh, yes my grace, I am so sorry will you please forgive me? You will be with them momentarily" she said as she snapped her fingers.

Sure enough a moment later we were in a giant room with eight women floating above us in red velvet cloaks.

The ones in the middle floated down in front of me and bowed, oh my god. How could I have forgotten that? I bowed back, when I looked up the women looked so very nervous.

"My lady, you need not bow to us"

"Why is everyone treating me like this? I would like to know what is wrong with me now!" I yelled then all the women floated down and were bowing to me.

"My lady, you are the white dragon"

"What!"

"The white dragon; the legend says that the white dragon has more power than any magical being in existence or than has ever been in existence. And also more power than all of us combined" she said looking around then added "And we are the superiors"

"Great, this just keeps getting better and better huh?"

"Do I not please you with this news?" she asked looking sheepishly at the ground.

"You will tell me why I seem to scare everyone and what your names are"

"I am Serena, the leader of the superiors"

"I am Sahara" the last one on the left said

"I am Suri" said the right of Sahara

"Scarlet" said one

"Sage" said another

"Saigon" followed Sage

"Sorrel" said another one of them, although I could tell which direction it had come from.

"My name is Sylvia" said the last one.

"So left to right, and tell me if I'm wrong; Sahara, Suri, Sorrel, Serena, Scarlet, Sage, Saigon, and Sylvia"

"Yes my lady" they all said in united.

"Okay, so now why is everyone so scared of me?"

"I hope I am not speaking out of turn my greatness, but we fear you because of all the power you wield. Here in the magical realm, status and respect is measured by magic. And your magic is higher than anyone has ever been, as much as I do not want to admit it; your power is greater than the power of everyone here, excluding you, multiplied by two. For that we respect you greatly. It is not you we fear, but your power"

"Okay, well thanks for explaining that, I think I understand now" I said smiling at her.

"You're welcome, I'm glad you understand" she said shyly

"So can you tell me my powers?" I asked

"Well yes, although you have many, they are all very rare, your powers are; Empathism, healing, commanding, levitating, absorbing powers, detecting danger, shape-shifting, invisibility, paralyzing, trapping souls, reflection, shielding, water walking, dream walking, time travel, draining powers, illusionism, transportation, intuition, silencing, demoralizing, and anything dragon related like breathing fire, flying, and you can shape-shift into a dragon as well. You can also summon dragon qualities" said Serena

"Wow, well how many is that exactly?"

"I think it's like 26; usually we can only have two at the most. So do you see now how special you are?"

"Yeah, I think so, and thanks" I said

"You're welcome my lady" they all said again in unison.

"Scott?" I asked finally noticing he wasn't with me.

"He didn't come here with you"

"He's not here?"

"No, he isn't. Would you like us to send for him?"

"No thank you, but I am here because of him"

"So what exactly do you need?"

"I wanted to know if he could drink from the fountain of eternal life . . . I have so much to learn and I really want him to be able to teach me everything he knows. He is my best friend and I believe that he could help me more than anyone else could"

"My lady, you do understand the possible consequences of us allowing this don't you?" asked Sage

"Yes I do"

"And you're sure you understand them?"

"Yes, more than I've ever understood anything"

"Then it shall be done"

"Really . . . thank you so much!"

"So you are pleased with this answer?" Asked Saigon

"Yes, of course!"

"We are glad to hear that" Said Serena as everyone muttered their agreements.

A moment later I was back at the fountain. Scott and Destiny were setting on the side of the fountain, holding hands and laughing. She looked so happy, and he looked even happier. As soon as the superiors saw this they left.

CHAPTER 45

"**H**ey" I yelled as loud as I could

"Oh hey" Scott said sounding surprised.

"So what are you guys talking about?" I asked as I walked up to them.

"Oh we were talking about the good times we used to have when we dated" Destiny said smiling

"Wait, you to dated?" I asked in complete shock and on the verge on full on rage.

"Yeah" she said like it was no big deal.

"Oh, um . . . okay" I said looking away.

"Are you okay? You don't look so good Mackenzie" Scott said as he made a move to stand up but sat back down when Destiny grabbed his arm.

"Gee thanks Scott, no I'm not. Can we please go?"

"Sure"

"Wait! We were in the middle of a conversation" Destiny said with an attitude.

"Oh, well the conversation's over." I said to her copying her attitude then pleading said to Scott "Come one, please"

"You're not going anywhere" She said as she shape-shifted into a giant phoenix, with astonishing red, yellow, orange, white and black feathers. The bird had to have been at least 15 feet tall.

"What kind of bird is that?"

"A phoenix" Scott replied in a hushed tone.

"Oh okay, well then bird brain, get ready to rumble"

"Sure thing dragon breath" "she said, although it was weird hearing her voice come out of the bird's beak.

That was the last straw. I shape-shifted into a giant pearly-white dragon that had; gigantic silver claws, white and silver wings, huge icy blue eyes, and a tail with silver spikes coming out of it.

Before I realized what had even happened she had morphed into a giant white dragon. Well I'm a fire phoenix so I have the advantage,

I flew over to her, clawed her back, legs and wings. But they haled. There was no way she could heal, but yet she did. Then she flew at me landed on my back and clawed my eyes, legs and back. Then all of the sudden I felt a sharp pain, then nothing.

At first I was just watching in awe and hoping Destiny had a chance. But then Mackenzie healed herself, clawed Destiny, and then snapped her neck. How could she have done that to someone? She's not a killer, and in hr dragon state, she has to be able to know what she's doing. Or maybe she didn't have control of her dragon state from the beginning. Either way she's dangerous and my mom was right, that's all I know and it's all I need to know.

"Mackenzie, you can stop now, she's dead. Please shift back to your human form" I yelled up at her, only to see her dragon look at me angrily and come running at me.

I didn't mean to kill her. But I didn't have any control; it was like I felt it but couldn't stop it from happening. I felt helpless in my dragon form. Wait, what's that over there? I turned to my left to see Scott waving his arms in the air and yelling at me. He was trying to get my attention that much was clear. And the next thing I know, I'm charging at him. I couldn't see what would happen. Just then a surge of power came through me and I was able to stop the dragon. Then I started falling and fast, but I couldn't scream, and before I knew it I hit the ground hard; and pain washed over me. Then everything went numb and blackness consumed me.

She stopped and then the dragon disappeared like it was just mist or an illusion of the wind. And she started falling, and she was falling fast, I ran to catch her but she hit the ground with an unusually loud thud. I knelt beside her to see if she was okay.

Her eyes were closed, her breathing shallow, and when I touched her skin I got badly burned. How could I help her and see if she is alive if I couldn't touch her? Then it hit me.

"Superiors, help me please. Mackenzie is hurt and I don't know how to help her" As I finished my sentence the superior's were there and already by her side.

"This is very unusual, can one of you try and shield and mover her?" asked Serena

The superior's tried their shields, levitation; transporting and every time the superior would fall to the ground weak. She was draining their powers, she was power resistant and she was draining their power, which meant their powers didn't work on her. Her power took it and wove it in with her and just made her stronger.

"What can we do?" I asked panicking

"Nothing, I'm afraid she will have to find her way back on her own" she said as we both looked down at her still body that lay on the cold ground.

CHAPTER 46

I was walking in what seemed like a desert, it was dry, hot and I couldn't see anything but dirt everywhere I looked. I looked around once more and saw something in the distance. I didn't care what it was as long as it could give me some shade. I walked and walked and walked toward what looked more and more like a small castle the closer I got to it. When I finally approached it I saw that I was right, it was a small castle. I opened one of the massive wooden doors and walked inside, thankful that it was cool inside. I looked around, and there was no one there. I wandered through the halls wondering who had lived here and why someone would put a castle in the middle of the desert anyways. I found a flight of stairs that led down, then another and another. I walked down every flight of stairs until I came upon a giant golden door. It was locked and the only way to open it was by magic. I stepped back and threw all the magic I could at it, strangely enough it came out as flames. But the doors opened and inside were 12 eggs. I walked up to them to get a better look, they were all so beautiful. They all appeared to have scales on the outside of them, but they were all different colors. In order from left to right the colors were; Electric blue, Light green, Fire red, Bright yellow, Gold, Silver, Pink, Purple, Caribbean green, Maroon, Teal, and Black. I walked up to the eggs and picked the golden one up, I felt drawn to all the eggs, I didn't know why but I was. When I started cradling the egg it started feeding on my dragon flame and started cracking. I sat the egg back down and stepped back; afraid it would break. It took me a moment to realize that the egg was hatching. When it was finished hatching it raised its tiny head up out of the egg and I saw that it was a dragon. It was a white dragon and had golden scaled scattered across its back, wings and head. It couldn't have been bigger than an iguana. It was so adorable, I could help but say "Awe" but when I did I scared the baby dragon and it ducked back into the bottom of the egg. I walked over to the egg, reached down into it and scooped the dragon up into both hands. It fed on my dragon flame once more and grew a little too where I could hold it like a baby. It seemed to purr in my arms as I played with it. I sat it down but it stayed by my side. I went over to the other eggs and used my dragon flame to pour fire onto them. They all hatched every one of them except the last one, the black one. They all looked the same. White colored scaled scattered across their bodies, the colored scales matched the color that was on their egg. It was both cool and cute; my guess was so that you knew what kind of dragon they were or something. I walked down the line to the black egg and used my dragon flame once more, it didn't work, I was afraid it was dead so I said "Little egg, you need to hatch, I want to see you. Please little dragon" and then it hatched. It was strange but my guess was that it followed what I said as a command. When it hatched it was all black, like a shadow. That's what its name was going to be "Shadow" I told him, he purred and jumped into my arms and I took it that he liked it.

I went to every dragon and named them according to their scales. The gold ones name was to be Guider. I named the electric blue one Current and the silver one Galaxy. The light green one was now Moss, the fire red one was Blaze, the bright yellow one is now Dancer. Teal was Breeze. Maroon is Blade, Caribbean is now Monk, purple was now Xena and I had decided to name the pink on Aphrodite.

I hollered for the dragons and we left but when we left the castle we were no longer in the desert, but a snow covered ground in a full blown blizzard.

I used my dragon flame to feed them and my shield to keep them warm and out of the snow. Shadow kept disappearing into a mist so I stopped worrying about if he would come back because I knew he would. I walked for miles and miles and was becoming increasingly tired, from the fatigue of walking and from maintaining a shield around the baby dragons. I was near passing out when I heard a small voice say "We can keep ourselves warm Arianna, we have a natural internal body heat so we can survive harsh conditions. It's okay, let the shield go" I look over at the pink dragon that was looking right at me. "Was that you who talked?" I asked her, "Yes" was the short and sweet reply.

"Are you sure you can keep warm?"

"Yes, we are. We have decided that our master needs to stay strong so we can protect her"

"I'm not your master though, I'm just Mackenzie"

This time Monk talked and he said "You know yourself as Mackenzie but your birth name is Arianna. You're a queen from a magic land and your bond with your land will be restored soon and you will remember everything. We can protect ourselves, we know much. We have been reincarnated over a thousand times and we know our strengths and weaknesses, you need not to protect us. You are our new master because you hatched us from our eggs; we have never known you're kind of magic, and we need now to feed from it. But we will not feed unless you are strong and well. So please master let the shield go. We can protect you from the harsh winter.

"Okay, but only if you are sure"

"We are" Monk said

"Okay" I told them as I dropped the shield and they floated to the ground. They each drew from my flame just enough so they were as tall as me; Galaxy and Blaze locked their wings above me so I was safe from the snow. Guider melted the snow before I stepped to keep my feet from getting frozen by the snow.

We walked this was until sun down and we found a cave and used it as shelter.

CHAPTER 47

She was dying. The longer she was asleep the faster her magic was fading. When her magic was all gone, she would die. Magic is in her blood, it's what keeps her moving, breathing, living and without it she's dead.

"What are we going to do when she comes back; if she comes back?" I asked worried about what the answer would be.

"Her power is out of control, we must make it leave her body" Said Serena as the others agreed

"But that will kill her!" I yelled at them all

"Not the way I have in mind" she said with a mysterious tone in her voice.

When I awoke the next day I was cold, and felt as if every muscle in my body was on fire and like my bones was concrete. I couldn't move; I couldn't even turn my head without having a sharp pain shoot down my spine.

"Help me, please. I can't move. I have to leave" I said breathlessly.

"We cannot help you, your magic is leaving you and soon we will be reborn into another egg. When our master dies, so do we" Said Guider.

"I'm not going to die, please. Help me" I pleaded with them

"We can't!" Shadow said followed by guider saying "I am sorry"

"Please, I need to live. I have to get back to my home, to my mom and dad, to my sister. Please, just help me"

"We can't. And you will meet them all soon enough, not the family you know, but your real family"

"What are you talking about? I know my sister is Natalya, and I know my mom is Geneva and my dad is; I don't know who he is" I said as reality hit me square in the face. To be honest I didn't know who any of my family was. How could I not even know my own family, maybe it would be best to just lay here forever?

As I let darkness wash over me I couldn't help but think 'is everything a lie'?

She had been asleep for a long time. I was about to give up hope when Mackenzie moaned and turned over. She looked at me and I couldn't help but feel like a part of me had been restored.

"Scott, I need water" she whispered in a hoarse voice.

"Okay, hold on" he said as I helped her onto the side of the fountain and before I could grab her, she had dived into it.

"Arianna get out of that fountain right now!" shouted Sage somewhere behind me.

I looked into the water, she was gone. "She's gone, where did she go?"

"I don't know, but I have a pretty good idea" said Serena in a dark voice

Let's just hope she isn't repeating his mistakes. I don't care how far she goes; she can't know her real father, he was a danger to us all and I cannot allow that once more. He needs to stay in the underworld.

Her mother made the mistake of trusting him. And I tried to warn her but it was too late. If she would have listened she would still be alive.

I was walking through the underworld when I came upon a black castle that looked like nothing more than a shadow. Yet somehow I was drawn to it. I walked in through the front doors and down multiple halls before I came upon a set of giant double doors. I pushed them open and he was there. The man I had been looking for when I didn't know I was. It was my father, king of the underworld.

"Hi dad" I said as I strolled in through the doors. Then I added 'Do you mind if I cast some light, I want to know what you look like" I asked boldly.

"Of course, am I so glad to finally meet you, you look so much like your mother" he said.

"I get that a lot from these old croaks"

"All the superiors, they have never been a friend to me either. What do you say you helped me get out of this prison and we go find your mother?" he said trying to make it into a joke.

I cast some light on him to see that he looked familiar. He had medium length, wavy black hair; that was as black as coal. Pale skin, chiseled features, he also had blue eyes as cold as ice, and he seemed to be in good shape. I couldn't help to think about where I had seen him before.

"Ok dad, so how do I get you out of here?" I asked.

"You say, "I release you and then I'm good to go where ever I please" he said with a twisted smile on his face.

"Ok. I release you" as I finished my last word he glowed and got off the throne and walked up beside me and said" let's go find your mother." And we were on our way.

We walked and walked for miles through the underworld until we came upon a white gate. I opened it and we walked through it. We walked until we came upon a white castle afloat on a massive cloud.

"So how do we get up there?" I asked.

"We fly" he said looking at me as if I was a child.

CHAPTER 48

We flew up to the castle and walked inside. There were servants who ran and disappeared into the walls as we walked by. We walked down a few halls before I realized that this was the same castle as the one in Nitoriah, only this one was all white and was floating on a cloud. The one in the dark, part of the underworld was also identical except for it being black and on a ground of black mist.

When we reached the throne room I pushed the doors open only to see my mother on a throne beside my sister. My mother was beautiful; she had beautiful bright curly blonde hair that was worn down. Her hair went half way down her back; she wore a diamond crown and had blue streaks through her hair. Her face looked like an angel; she had fair skin, bright blue eyes, and pink lips. She was wearing a pure white dress that was strapless and had a long skirt that flowed around her. The front of the skirt was shorter in the front and came up past her knees, she was bare foot. She wore a wide golden belt and held a staff which had a diamond dragon placed on the very top of it.

My sister looked exactly like me; apparently I had a twin sister. She was gorgeous. She had long wavy light brown hair that was as long as our mothers. She had a smaller diamond tiara placed upon her head, she was also fair skinned, had big brown eyes, and pale pink lips and cheeks. She had white streaks through her hair; which was the only indicator that told people who was who. She was wearing a pure white dress like a goddess would wear, she was also bare foot. And she sat there like she owned the place" well she did, kind of.

"Hello mom" I said as she just stared at me.

"Yes, hello darling" my dad said with disgust in his voice.

"You shouldn't be here Daniel" she finally said.

"Oh honey, you always were stubborn even when you knew you wouldn't win" he spat at her.

"There is always hope" she said calmly

"Bull crap there is!" he shouted making everyone jump.

"Please, do not do this right now, I would like to finally meet my father and sister" said my sister as she looked at my mother, who looked back and agreed "Ok, since my daughter Maria wants a chance to meet her sister we will have a feast. Besides I need a chance to talk to you in private, Daniel" said my mom before she stood and left the throne room, and my dad followed.

I looked over to her and she stood, and ran over to me and hugged me.

"I'm I missing something? We just broke into your castle and your hugging me?"

"You're my sister" she said smiling.

"Ok this is weird. I never knew I had a twin"

"You don't, I'm the positive half of you. You were to dangerous when we were one so the superior's come to our mother and begged her to do what had to be done. She did. She kept me here and safe from you, and gave father the bad half. She thought he would be pleased but he wanted his full daughter not half of her. She placed you in Nitoriah, faked her own death and lock own dad away. All to keep you safe and away from the truth"

"Why? I'm I not dangerous" I yelled as a window exploded.

"Now that we are close, you are even more powerful. And that makes you a threat. But I beg of you to take me back. I hate it here; all I ever hear is you have to do this, you have to do that and I never have any time for myself anymore!"

"Well I hate it everywhere I go!"

"Well then that's even more of a reason"

"Okay" I said as I summoned my dragon essence and pulled my good half back into my soul. I could feel the power running through my veins. I felt it in every breath I took; I felt the power and knew I wouldn't let it go.

I walked out of the castle, blasting anyone and everyone and anyone who tried to restrain me, with fire. As I left the castle all I heard was screaming, panic, and people screaming words of hate; which I now fed on.

I went back to the fountain to find Scott standing over it looking down and the superiors consulting amongst themselves. I cleared my throat and everyone jumped.

"Arianna, you're back" said Sage

"And with more power than before, and since you old hags are starting to bug me, say goodbye to your final breath" I said as I threw one hand up and Saigon burst into flames.

"My sister, my baby sister! What did you do?" Sage screamed and started crying.

"Why don't you join her" I said as I threw my hand up once more and she exploded into a pile of ash.

"Arianna, I'm warning you, stop this at once or you are going to do something you will regret!" screamed Serena

"And I'm warning you; back off or I will continue and leave you alive to relish in your failure of keeping them all safe!"

"Stop this now Arianna! I will not ask you again. There might not be as many of us but there are enough of us to get you into custody" said Serena

"How dare you challenge me!" I yelled in pure rage. I turned to Scarlet and snapped my fingers and her head snapped all the way around in one clean motion. Then I turned to Suri and waved my hand as she was torn apart limb by limb.

"My cousin, how dare you!" Sorrel said as she charged me and I jumped on her and snapped her neck.

"Anyone else want to challenge me? Sylvia? Sahara, what about you oh brave and might Serena?" I said laughing hysterically.

"Mackenzie, you need to stop this right now!" Scott screamed, I looked over at him and he fell to the ground twitching. I wasn't going to kill him; just play with him for a little while. He laid there on the ground writhing in pain for about an hour before I let him go, more out of boredom than niceness.

Drawing by Monica Jenkins

CHAPTER 49

I made myself a portal and was instantly in my castle, of Nitoriah. I walked down the halls and everyone that walked up to me found themselves being smashed against the concrete walls of the castle. I walked all the way to the throne room, opened the doors to find Artemis, Natalya and all of their advisors in the middle of a meeting about me.

I walked up toward the throne; every time someone looked at me I twisted my hand and they found themselves on the ground with a broken neck. "Ah, my dearest sister and her dad" I said standing in front of the thrones which they were setting on and making a mocking curtsey.

"What are you doing?" Demanded Natalya

"What I should have done a long time ago when you to kidnapped me!" I shouted.

"We did no such thing Mackenzie" said Artemis

"Oh brother dearest, why don't you call me by my real name?" I said sarcastically

"What are you talking about?" He demanded

"You know what I'm talking about; now say my real name or your precious daughter will be dragon kibble! And tell her the truth, how you have been lying to her and stealing her magic while she is asleep you were born without any!!! Go ahead, TELL HER!!!" I screamed and the top of my lungs

"Okay, okay, she is telling the truth" he said looking at Natalya. He then added "I have no powers so I take yours; I feed off your magic. And her real name is Arianna; I know this because she is my sister"

"You're lying, both of you! Please tell me you are lying!" Natalya said with fear in her eyes then added in a whispered tone "Please" and then burst into tears.

"We're telling the truth, and your dear daddy's name isn't really Artemis it's actually Richard"

"Now I know you're both lying! My dad's name is Artemis not Richard!"

"No my daughter she is telling the truth, my name is actually Richard. When we were kids, I sent her away and she nearly, our mother Mariana faked her own death to keep Arianna safe. She also split her soul, and kept the two halves away from each other all these years. I thought she was dead. I left her in the woods with the dragons when she was an infant. But the dragons were being hunted and didn't want the man to harvest their powers when he caught them; and when they found her they realized she was helpless and gave her their magic. There were 12 dragons. She had each of their powers. She had the dragon flame from the fire dragon, the dragon essence from the wise dragon, the powers of the earth dragon, water dragon, spirit dragon, shadow dragon, sun dragon, love dragon, healing dragon, war dragon, guardian dragon and the air dragon."

Natalya looked at him in disbelief and looked like she was still trying to process what he had just said. Then she replied "You left your sister infant in the woods, expecting hr to die, and now she is trying to kill everyone!" calmed herself and then added "You have lied to me my entire life and I want you to return my powers, and then leave me alone. I am not staying her bundled up in these lies. I must leave" and then she got up and left the room.

"Do you see what've you've done?" he yelled at me.

"Don't get your knickers in a twist, you've had it coming from the start" I said as I sat down in the throne she had just vacated and threw one leg up on the arm rest and made myself more comfortable. Then I added "You really shouldn't lied to her you know"

"She is the only daughter I have and ever will have! And now I have lost her because you thought it was necessary to get revenge!" he said as he collapsed into his throne and started crying.

I got up and crossed the throne room and opened the door, and without bothering to turn and face him I said "You have another daughter, and a son. They're twins."

"Where?" he asked his voice both hopeful and muffled by tears.

"In Valorence, your mate is also there. She knows about your true identity, and she isn't very happy about it. But she still waits for you"

"So they are alive and well? All of them?" he asked setting on the edge of his seat although he already knew my answer. I said "Yes" then stepped out of the throne room and shut the door in one fluid motion.

CHAPTER 50

I ran down the hall and to my room. When I was finished packing and about to open a portal there was a knock at my door. I walked over and it. Mackenzie was standing there and as I looked at her she walked right in and said "My dear niece, I am sorry you had to witness all of that. I just now found out who I really am an hour ago and I was in disbelief, I am sorry I threatened you. You must be tired of the lies as well though" she finished her sentence as she walked over and sat down on my bed, right next to my suitcase. She pointed to the luggage and said "If this is what it's come to then why not just come with me?"

"Because how do I know you won't lie to me too?"

"Because I am also tired of all the lies, and why in the world would I keep them going?" she said looking a bit offended.

"I don't know, I am sorry Mackenzie" I said feeling ashamed

"Don't be sorry, I understand how you feel. I am going through the same thing, why don't you just join me and help me stop the lies we both hate so much" she said as she closed the distance between us and gave me a big hug.

"I will go with you Mackenzie, I will help you stop the lies; just tell me how" I said making my decision.

"Come with me back to my home in Mandonia" she said getting a bit excited.

"Where's that at?" I asked, realizing I've never heard of it.

"It's a planet outside of the five magic kingdoms. It's on the edge of the magic dimension. It is beautiful there"

"Okay let's go" I said as she opened a portal.

When we got through the portal it was exactly like I remembered it. Big, beautiful and healthy bright green trees, covered with flowers. Fields of flowers everywhere you looked, mountains with beautiful white mountaintops. There was a lake of to my left, Lake Larone. The sun was setting and it cast a mesmerizing color onto the water. I looked back at Natalya who was smiling and looking around; my guess was she was taking everything in.

I grabbed her arm and all but drug her up to the castle which sat on top of a hill. We were walking on a dirt road and a few minutes later we reached the front steps of the castle. When we walked inside I looked around and was happy to be home, except everywhere I looked there were blood splatters. There was a war here and everyone, all of my friends and most of my family got slaughtered. I looked back again to Natalya who now looked sad.

"It's okay, we can get this place cleaned up in no time at all" I said as cheerful as possible; but it didn't work.

"A war, Richard had told my father where to find me. My father is the king of the underworld and he sent his immortal slaves to retrieve me like I was some kind of animal. I lost a lot of people I loved that day; family, friends, play mates. Elderly people, mothers, fathers, brother and sister were all murdered as well as children and babies, some only a few months old. I lost my own baby brother that day. Everyone who died either died because they were fighting back so they wouldn't be able to take me, or trying to keep my location a secret. And some were murdered for fun I suppose. I was horrible."

"I am so sorry Mackenzie; I hope nothing like that ever happens to anyone ever again."

"I do to. It was a great loss; we lost many loyal, pure people that day" I agreed.

"I am so sorry about what happened" she said looking truly sorry.

"As am I" I said and then looked at the floor and started to cry.

I took her arm and led her to her room; the room that was once mine.

"You can have this room, mine is right across the hall. If you need anything just yell, I will keep my door opened okay?"

"Okay and thank you so much for being so kind to me, I know it can't be easy" she said looking guiltily at the floor.

"We have both had our share of loses, and it is no trouble. You are family and family looks after one another in times of need" I said smiling at her.

"Thank you again, and this room is beautiful"

"You're welcome. This room was once mine you know. Anyways the bathroom is on the other side of the bed, your closet is right there" I said pointing to the door at the end of her bed. Then I added "If you want different clothes just say what you would like to wear and it will appear on the bottom rack on a hanger, okay?"

"Okay, and whose crowns are those?" she asked pointing to the ones lined up on the dresser.

"They are now yours princess" I said curtsying.

"Oh, thank you so much"

"You're very welcome" I said as I turned to leave.

"Wait where are you going?" she asked panicky.

"I am going to change and then I am going to start cleaning this place up" I said as she smiled and added "Well I am going to help, this place could use some nice decorating" I winced; my mother had decorated this castle. But even when she started laughing I joined in.

I left the room and walked across the hallway; before I opened the doors I felt something, a life force. Someone was in that room, and whoever it was, their essence was familiar.

I pushed open the doors and braced myself for an ambush. But instead I found a torn apart room. I walked through what was once my mother's room. I searched the room for life, I knew someone was in there, but there was no one a person could hide. Then I heard crying, there were however plenty of places to hide a baby.

CHAPTER 51

I started flipping furniture back over and finally made my way into a room branched off the main one. The room that was once my brother's nursery, I looked in the crib; nothing. I looked under the crib and again nothing. I looked under every piece of furniture I could find. I got up off the floor and looked to the other side of the room, there was a door. A closet, I walked over to it and pulled open the doors. And there at the bottom of the closet in the corner all wrapped up was a baby boy. I picked him up and pulled off the cover that was around him, sure enough there was a crescent moon shaped scar on his right ankle. The exact same scar in the exact same place my brother had.

"Natalya! I found him, he's not dead after all" I yelled as I heard her trip and fall as she came running through the door. I giggled then added "And make sure you are careful, I'm in the back room."

"Okay hold on" she said and a moment later she came through the doorway.

"Look, this is my brother, he's not dead. I don't know how he survived, but the point is he's not dead!" I said excitedly as the baby just stared up at us.

"Oh my goodness, he is such a cute baby!" she squealed.

"I know, so how are we going to take care of him" I asked her as I looked back down at him.

"Well we need to get this place cleaned up first, wait does anyone live here anymore?"

"I don't know, maybe"

"Why don't we go look?"

I bundled him back up into his covers and held him close to me. I wasn't about to lose him again. We walked to the village it seemed that it was like a mile down the road. When we first approached the village it seemed like no one was there, but after I walked through the barrier, that was put up to protect the people, I felt hundreds of souls. There were hundreds of people still here.

We walked to Main Square and I stood and I stood on the side of the fountain that was placed there for the people to gather fresh water, cleared my voice and announced "My name is Arianna, I am your princess, I have returned to watch to watch over my people and re-bond with my land. My land welcomes me home and I hope with all my heart that my people do the same. I know I have left you, but it was not my best choice. The crops were dying, and I was afraid you all would as well. I apologize greatly. But I need your help. You see my baby brother, Prince Lance the one we all thought was dead is right here" I said holding him up in the air for a moment and then holding him close to me once more. "I need help repairing the castle and I also need someone with a pure heart to watch my dearest brother until the castle if restored and I can take care of him myself. Anyone who is willing to take a job in the castle I will pay 3 pounds once a week. The crops will grow back healthier than ever before. And there will be no more pain or suffering. I can promise you all of that. But I need help from you all" as I finished people started pouring out of their houses and hiding places and were crowding me.

About an hour later, I had a table set up and people employed. I had hired about nine cooks, thirty three maids, twelve repair men, twenty eight painters, seven decorators, a treasurer, a new accountable, an assistant, two elderly women who begged to watch after my brother because their own kids have died. I hired anyone and everyone who wanted or needed a job.

The next day when I walked outside people were showing up for work. I opened the door and people were getting to work. The cooks were making food for the workers; they were making sandwiches, lemonade, and slicing fresh fruit.

I walked through the castle and was pleased to find that the walls were no longer covered in blood, the old dirty drapes were gone, there was nothing left in the castle except the kitchen ware, and the castle itself.

I walked up to Natalya's room to find her curled up in a fetal position on her bed. I walked over to her, sat down beside her and said in a calm and caring voice "My dear niece, you are here, we have found a lost relative, we are once more a kingdom, and there is much to celebrate why are you not happy?"

"Because I miss my dad, and Lance is a Deidra. He is feeding off your power. When you first walked into the castle his spirit felt your presence, re-entered his body and he brought himself back to life. His body has been here since the accident, he was in the middle of decomposition when he was brought back. He is dead, and if you allow him to live he will only bring death and destruction to everyone.

"Lies, Lies! All of it, he is not dead, he didn't die and he will not bring death to everyone! If this is how you think you shall be banned from this kingdom, I just found him and I will not lose him again!"

"It's true!" she yelled at me in a harsh voice

"How do you know?" I asked in disgust

"Because I am an oracle and I know this, for when I touched him yesterday I saw all of his soul's memories. He died and he feeding of you magic. He is bonding to you, you have to kill him"

"I can't" I said as I fell to the ground and started crying.

A moment later I got up on the ground, straightened my clothes then dusted them off and I left the room to find my brother. I searched all over the castle before I went back to my room to see if he was in his nursery. When I opened the doors the first thing I saw was my beautiful bed, it was so gold colored comforter that was lined with white and had white lace around the edges of the cover. The pillows were all white with gold lining; the bed was a polished wooden four post bed. The walls were cream colored.

The floor was all wooden and was brilliantly polished. They even put in three new dressers, a vanity, new closet doors, and placed white fur rugs on both sides of the bed and a larger one in the center of the room.

I walked toward my brother's nursery and saw that his room was done in an ocean blue; he had pure white crib, with a blue blanket that matches the color of the walls. He also white fur rugs. One larger one under his crib which was in the center of the room, he had another fur rug in the front of his closet door. He had a brand new changing station, a play area, and lots of stuffed toys, and had four protective amulets tied to his crib, one on each side. There was a rocking chair in the corner of the room next to a shelf which held at least a hundred children's books.

I looked down in his crib and he was asleep. He was so peaceful, I couldn't kill him. I wouldn't kill him, he was my brother. I reached down and scooped him into my arms, walked over to the rocking chair and I rocked him back and forth for about an hour before he woke up due to the sound of glass breaking. Someone down stairs had broken one of the new windows.

"It's okay lance, it was just a noise. Go back to sleep" I said looking down at him as he drifted back off to sleep. And I suddenly felt weak. He was feeding off my powers. I got up out of the rocking chair walked back over to his crib and laid him back down, covered him up and kissed his forehead.

We lived in our new castle for a few months before things started to change. Lance was feeding off everyone's powers. He was draining theirs powers to fast and was taking too much and died. My pet dragons returned and I was working on training them to fight. There was a battle coming up it was going to be massive and I was determined to win.

CHAPTER 52

I hadn't heard from Arianna in months, it's been almost a year now since she disappeared. And I had the feeling she was coming back. The night before I had vision that she was going to start a war, and I couldn't tell the superior's. They would try to kill her after what she'd done to them. I'd have to find a way to end the war before it started. I searched very kingdom in every dimension and found no sign of her. Today I'm in royal library in Nitoriah trying to find somewhere that I've missed.

I had been looking for at least three hours before I finally found what I was looking for. The map of the five magic dimensions, I was half through the book when something caught my eye it said

> *There is a sixth kingdom spoken of in legend it was called Mandonia. It was where the queen Mariana, the first queen and King Daniel, the first king originated. They had met and started a kingdom there, but when they were ambushed in their own home they moved and started over on a new planet which was named Nitoriah. They left behind the only way to ever be able to stop the evil one. The white dragon; for white is the hottest flame and the white dragon is the most dangerous thing*

out there. The white dragon on exists in myth but it is said that one day she will return and end what she started years ago; A war to enslave all creatures. Queen Marianna was assisted by her husband in stopping the white dragon. The powers of the white dragon were split between the two, the pure and good side was bestowed upon Marianna and the dark and evil side was placed on Daniel. For king Daniel begged for his wife to be good. The only way to stop her is to reunite the lost lovers so they can free the staff of light and stop the white dragon.

I knew there was another place I couldn't have checked. But that would have to wait; I needed to find Marianna and Daniel first.

We were still arguing about Arianna when we heard an explosion and then yelling. Then we know that she had consumed the other half of her and we were in trouble. He each held a piece of the staff. But that was only two pieces, we needed the third one. Which was in Arianna, and there was no way we were going to be able to return to Mandonia, not now not ever. The land did not welcome us. And every living thing on that planet was in danger as long as she was there. There was no way to stop her; ever.

We needed to prepare for war, a big one.

I was training my dragons once more to make sure they knew what they were doing when one of my many soldiers ran up to me, saluted and said "Ma'am the ogre's are ready for battle. As are the Giants, Sprites, Cyclops', Fairies, Nymphs, Phoenix's, Elves', Dark angel's, Banshee's, Brownie's, Demons, Vampire's, Lions, Wolves, Bears, Succubi, Unicorns, Pegasus', Sirens, Centaur's, Minotaur's, Griffin's and the Hydra's"

"Which ones are not ready soldiers?"

"Ma'am the harpies, manticores, pixies, kelpies, imps, incubi, satyrs, trolls, shee, wendigos, yetis and the wraiths"

"Tell them to hurry and give me a count of how many of each we have total"

"Yes ma'am" said the soldier as he marched away.

The war was almost here and my dragons were trained. I will win this battle believe me on that one. A moment later the soldier returned and handed me a piece of paper which read.

*5,000 giants, sprites, elves, brownies, vampires, centaurs *7,000 Cyclops', unicorns, Pegasus *300 bears, wolves, lions *700 succubi, nymphs *6,000 fairies *6,500 sirens *500 banshees *10,000 dark angels *8,000 hydras *50,000 Minotaur's *70,000 phoenix's *80,000 demons and griffins

I looked at the soldier and said "Tell them I am very pleased, and let me know when all creatures are ready"

"Yes ma'am I will be right back" he said as he turned and ran away. I looked back at the rising sun and thought about the battle that was about to unfold, couldn't help but smile at the thought.

The soldier returned once more; he was starting to aggravate me. He handed me another piece of paper and said "They are all here and awaiting your command my queen" before he turned and disappeared.

I looked down at the paper and read: *100 shee, wendigos *250 yetis *600 harpies *700 imps *900 manticores *1,000 pixies, kelpies *3,000 wraiths *6,000 satyrs, trolls *7,000 incubi

We were for sure going to win. I walked up a flight of stairs to my room, opened up the doors to the balcony and walked out there. I looked down over my vast army of soldiers, and creatures and couldn't help but smile. Now it's time for my big motivational speech.

"My friends, we have been slaves to the powerful rulers of the dimensions for too long. I am also a ruler but I only wish for peace and equality, not power. The enemies today, the ones we are to face have tried to repress us for too long! I no longer want to be defined by how much power I have or if my power is their standards! Power is for one's self, to make us feel important not to label us in social class. We are equal we are all given our powers from the same place; we are all gifted, so why should we be divided? The answer is we should not! We, us magical beings are tired of being judged. And you my friends, the magical creatures on the dimensions, I know you are tired of being forced to take jobs we refuse, I know you suffer in silence because you fear no one will listen and that you will be judged! But follow me and win this battle not for me but for yourselves. I can't promise everyone will make it, because there will be loses. But we are fighting today for equality, peace, and hope for a better life. I ask of you, think of you kids, your friends and family. How being treated like this affects them, they do not want to live like this and neither do we, after today we will no longer have to live like this. So my friends I ask of you one last thing, go out there today and fight; fight not with revenge in mind, or a grudge in your heart. Fight with the hope that tomorrow will make the lives of your loved ones better, the hope that everyone will be equal, the hope that we all will live along side one another and be one!!!" I shouted as everyone burst into cheers.

CHAPTER 53

When we reached our battle field which was in Nitoriah; in the field where I first fought Sicilia, we prepared for war. Then just as I suspected the army that my parents had got together came charging out of the woods in an attempt to ambush us; my creatures and soldiers charged back and the war had begun.

I climbed onto the back of blade, the war dragon. And we soared through the sky torching dressed in armor; which was brought to me by the ogres. They were fighting, clawing, and eating everyone who charged them. Would any of them learn not to charge at a dragon? I guess not, besides the swords, claws, and fire seemed kind of peaceful to me.

We all fought until there were no more soldiers that fought for the opposite team. We had lost probably a 1,000 people total. It was no major loss. The only ones left were my parents. I called off my army and dismissed them. When they were gone I climbed down from blade and dismissed him as well. When everyone was gone I walked over to them and said "It looks like I won this war, so is this part where you try to take that last piece of the staff and kill me"

"No Arianna it is not" said Marianna

"Okay so why don't you hand over Nitoriah or I can take that from you as well"

"It is yours" said my dad

"Okay so what's the catch? You try to get me to go into the castle and when I do you ambush and kill me? Don't you think I'm smarter than that?" I said pretending to be offended.

"Yes, we know you are smarter than that, but you aren't smarter this" said Marianna as I felt a sharp pain in my back.

I turned around to see Anthea standing there, I torched her before I collapsed and black out.

CHAPTER 54

I awoke in a daze and in what looked like a hospital. I looked around and saw Geneva in a chair beside me, and Scott standing against a wall at the end of my bed.

I looked over at my mom and said "Where am I? Did they hand over Nitoriah?"

"What are you talking about honey? And you are in the hospital, how are you feeling?"

"Very sore, what happened?" I demanded

"You were in a car wreck honey; you've been in a coma for the past year and a half. The doctor said your were starting to be responsive and that we should be come see you"

"What that can't be right. I wasn't in a coma"

"Yes you were honey, you broke an arm, your ankle and dislocated to disks in you back, they had to perform surgery but they said you'd be fine. You've been healing quite fast actually"

"What?" I said right before I fell back asleep

I awoke that night when my mom started shaking me. I looked at her and she was smiling "What mom"

"We get to take home; they said you are well enough to go home. But when we get you home you have to stay in bed, and they are calling your school. You can't go back this month, I'm sorry. But you won't be able to see Brittany or any of your other friends unless they come over"

"Oh, okay. Then let's go home mom" I said as the nurse brought in a wheel chair, I couldn't get a good look at her but she looked like, she looked like Marianna from my dream. But that couldn't be right. I must have seen her and remember her face and made some crazy fantasy with her in it. Maybe I do need more rest after all.

When we got home mom helped me up to my room and helped me get in bed. I fell asleep when she left the room; I woke up the next morning and looked over to my dresser. And setting on my dresser was a diamond dragon, the one from my dream. Maybe it wasn't a dream after all.